Also by Ellis Blackwood

The Samuel Pepys Mysteries
Book 0.5: Mr Pepys's Stolen Diaries
(via ellisblackwood.com)
Book 1: The Brampton Witch Murders
Book 2: The Plague Doctor Murders
Book 3: The Coffee House Murders
Book 4: The King's Court Murders (January 2025)

Scan the QR code for social links and website.

The Plague Doctor Murders

The Samuel Pepys Mysteries Book 2

Ellis Blackwood

Vintage Mystery Press

ISBN: 978-1-0687027-1-6

Cover design, editorial & historical fact-checking: Tim Brown, A.S.C. (Rtd).

Additional editing: Charles Johnston.

Cover illustration licensed from shutterstock.com.

For Regan, my favourite little raspberry blower.

Contents

Chapter One

Return to London

Ensconced in the Huntingdonshire countryside many miles from London, Abby and Jacob had no idea they had escaped the most devastating fire the city had ever witnessed. "I was obliged to bury my Parmesan cheese in the garden," Mr Pepys told them, mopping his brow at the memory. The dense wheel of cheese had been simply too heavy to carry to safety.

Samuel Pepys was returning to London by horse-drawn coach from Brampton. Seated opposite him were Jacob Standish, his personal inquisitor, and Abigail Harcourt, his young housemaid whom he had allowed to aid Standish in a recent witchcraft investigation.

Abby, 19, wore a frayed linen dress with a woollen shawl and bonnet, all in cream. Her red hair was tied back, and her piercing turquoise eyes suggested a fierce intellect, which she had become adept at hiding, for fear of irritating boorish gentlemen above her station.

Jacob, three years her senior, was twice her size, thick-set, with unruly dark eyebrows that met in the middle. His doublet and coat were plain, and his felt hat sat lopsidedly on a periwig that had seen better days. He brought to mind an outsized puppy.

Mr Pepys? He looked immaculate, naturally. The very essence of a gentleman in charge of his own destiny. Yet there was something about his general disposition - the flushed, rounded cheeks, the eager expression - that spoke of joy and humanity within, not often found in men of his standing.

The two-day journey had begun in high spirits. Pepys's sister, Paulina, had been absolved of all the charges of witchery laid against her, thanks to Abby and Jacob, which filled Samuel with delight. That they had succeeded in unmasking a murderer and proving Paulina's innocence, despite their backgrounds as a servant and a failed purser's apprentice, was cause alone for celebration.

However, something appeared to be troubling Pepys.

Abby and Jacob had departed London for Brampton on the day the fire started: Sunday 2nd September, 1666. Pepys had joined them a week later, having witnessed first-hand the devastation the fire had wrought on his precious city.

It was clear that those memories had taken their toll. Pepys seemed distracted, and his customary bright-eyed disposition was replaced, as they jolted through ruts on the dried-mud road, with a drained and baleful demeanour.

"Sir," said Jacob, noticing the malaise. "Pray tell me what troubles you."

"It did seem as if Heaven itself were on fire," his employer replied, blankly staring.

Pepys recalled the panic as a fierce east wind fanned the flames towards the heart of the walled medieval city. Belongings were thrown into the streets, where they piled in the gutters, or were tossed into the River Thames in the hope of evading the flames. When the fire reached the warehouses on the north bank of the Thames, the oils and gunpowder stored there began to explode, creating an earthly version of Hell.

Pepys moved his best goods by cart to a friend's property in Bethnal Green, having buried his most expensive foodstuffs dressed only in his nightshirt. Afterwards, he had lived in constant fear that his house on Seething Lane, less than half a mile from the fire's starting point on Pudding Lane, would be consumed by the flames. God – and the wind direction – had proved to be his saviours.

In his work as Clerk of the Acts to the Navy Board, Pepys acted as an advisor to King Charles II and his brother James, Duke of York. On the day the fire started, he recalled travelling by river to Whitehall Palace, where the court resided, to warn His Majesty of a potential catastrophe. He suggested that houses in the fire's path be demolished, to halt its progress. The King had considered this a fine idea and ordered him to relay the same to the Lord Mayor, Thomas Bludworth.

Pepys narrowed his eyes. "When at last I found the Lord Mayor in Cannon Street, he looked like a man spent, with a handkerchief about his neck. To the King's message, he cried, like a fainting woman, 'Lord, what can I do? I am spent and the people will not obey me. I have been pulling down houses but the fire overtakes us faster than we can do it.'"

On learning of Bludworth's capitulation, the King and the Duke of York took charge of the firefighting effort themselves. Pepys recalled seeing the Duke joining a line of men with leather buckets, dousing the flames, and almost paying with his life when a building collapsed behind him.

After the fire leap-frogged the River Fleet and headed for Westminster and Whitehall, Charles retreated with his court to the safety of Hampton Court Palace, leaving James in charge.

Pepys recalled visiting the royal dockyard at Woolwich, from which distant vantage point the entire city appeared to be ablaze. The grim cloud of black smoke above the panorama of flames seemed to fill the sky like a permanent midnight.

Eventually, on Thursday, the fifth day of the conflagration, the flames abated. The wind died down and firefighters – some press-ganged into action – blew up enough wooden houses, sufficiently distant from the fire's path, that they deprived the flames of fuel. "Devastation remained," Pepys sighed.

Four-fifths of the walled city, he estimated, with its narrow streets and wooden buildings, lay razed to the ground. Despite the desolation, only half a dozen citizens were reported to have perished, although thousands were now homeless.

The thriving shopping street of Cheapside was gone, Pepys told Abby and Jacob, as was the ornate Exchange marketplace, where merchants once met and bartered. The lead roof of St Paul's cathedral had melted and flowed like lava down the streets, as the building beneath it collapsed.

At the end of these tragic recollections, Pepys wrung his hands and bowed his head. Jacob did the same, and his hat fell off. Abby, in tears, picked it up for him.

"Sir," Jacob addressed his mentor. "Are you aware… Did my house on Strand Lane survive the fire?"

Pepys exhaled, reached across and patted Jacob's thigh. "Fear not, Mr Standish. The fire did not reach even Temple Bar, thanks to the work of so many brave souls. Your house on Strand Lane still stands, rest assured."

Abby wiped her eyes with a dirty sleeve. "Master Pepys, what will become of London now?"

Pepys rose from the slouch that had overcome him. "The city has thrived for hundreds of years, Abigail, and it will thrive for many hundreds more, long after we are turned to dust. We must view this catastrophe as an opportunity. An opportunity for great men to make their names in the rebuilding of the city, such that it shall become the envy of the rest of the world."

Jacob found himself applauding. "Sir, your words will be an inspiration to all of London."

Pepys blushed and smiled to himself.

"When we return," Jacob said, "I would like to visit my house to check on my possessions, that they have not been damaged by smoke."

Pepys shook his head. "Nay, there is not the time, Mr Standish. I will assign a boy to the task on your behalf. Your attention lies elsewhere."

The younger man perked up. "Our next investigation, sir? I feared we may be put out to pasture, having investigated the witchery in Brampton."

Pepys almost choked. "Good heavens, nay, your work as my personal inquisitor has barely begun! I have already in mind a most perplexing case, which may baffle even you..."

Chapter Two

The Plague Doctor

P epys went on to outline the inquisitors' next investigation as their coach jolted through the night.

As Clerk of the Acts, Samuel Pepys was responsible for the administration of the royal dockyards: on the River Medway at Chatham in Kent; at Portsmouth on the south coast; and in London's rapidly expanding suburbs, at Woolwich and at Deptford.

From this last-mentioned had reached his ears a fearful tale indeed.

One of the pursers at Deptford was a fellow named Robert Drake, with whom Pepys had dined on occasion. Their roles were similar – though, as Pepys assured them, his own was of far greater importance. He had taken a liking to Drake, who possessed a keen head for figures. Pepys admired the young man's inquisitive nature and thirst for learning, seeing in him a shared devotion to the pursuit of knowledge – a quality he held in the highest regard. (He recognised the same trait in Abby and hoped that, under his guidance, Jacob might one day develop the same.)

Pepys confessed to his inquisitors that he had been shaken to the core when news arrived from Deptford that Robert Drake was in fear for his life. A black-cloaked figure, dressed as a plague doctor, had been seen prowling the dockyard under cover of night.

The figure - presumably a man, since the notion it might be a woman seemed unthinkable - wore the distinctive leather hood with glass eye-holes that concealed the entire head, shielding the wearer from the poisonous miasma thought to carry the plague. Most unsettling of all was the long, leather, beak-like protuberance extending from the mask, its tip packed with scented herbs to purify the air. The grotesque beak gave the wearer the ominous appearance of a giant crow, a sight that unnerved even the hardiest souls.

Plague doctors in such garb had become a familiar sight during the previous year and into this one, as the pestilence lingered. Since spring, however, the death toll had lessened, and London had, for the most part, begun to recover its usual rhythm.

The night before he had ridden to Brampton, Pepys had been informed that Humphrey Wilkes, an able seaman and close friend of Robert Drake, had discovered a chilling sight scrawled in paint upon his door: a black cross and the words, 'LORD HAVE MERCY UPON HIM.'

Such markings were dreadfully familiar, seen countless times during the plague. They were painted on the doors of houses whose occupants were infected – though the cross was usually red, not black, and the inscription would read, 'LORD HAVE MERCY UPON US.'

Wilkes's message appeared personally targeted at him – and to foretell his demise.

But Wilkes was not a man to be trifled with, Pepys noted. Though only in his early thirties, he had served in the navy for many years. He fought in the first Dutch war of the early 1650s, as well as the Spanish war that ended in 1660. Wilkes lost an eye during the capture of Jamaica from the Spanish in 1655, when a galleon's cannonball ripped through the bulwark he was defending, sending wooden shards flying.

"What has this to do with Robert Drake?" Jacob asked.

"Wilkes was found most grievously slain," Pepys replied. "Shot betwixt the eyes in his own house, and a plague doctor seen departing."

"And Drake?" asked Abby.

"Did discover of late upon his door, a black cross and the words, 'LORD HAVE MERCY UPON HIM,'" replied Pepys. Then, with a most grave expression, he turned to Jacob and clasped his hands. "Mr Standish, I fear greatly for my friend's life. You must save him."

Jacob was familiar with the royal docks, having worked at Woolwich dockyard as a purser's apprentice. There was a confident glint in his eye. "Sir, rest assured, you will not regret placing your trust in me. We triumphed in Brampton and we shall do likewise in Deptford."

Having stayed overnight at the King's Arms in Stevenage - the same inn in which Abby and Jacob had rested on their way to Brampton - the party arrived at Seething Lane on the night of Thursday the 13th of September. All were grateful that the ceaseless shaking of their bones, and the numbing of their buttocks on the hard coach seating, had come to an end.

Pepys's house was within the Navy Board's estate, a stone's throw from his office, and set behind ornamental gardens. Unlike the poorer residences that had perished in the fire, it was constructed over three floors of red brick and had pretty leaded windows. Opposite, the Church of St Olave's hourly bell chimed the rhythm to Pepys's day.

The kitchen maid, Mary Blythe, curtsied and took Pepys's hat and coat as he entered, did the same for Jacob, and grinned at Abby, who trailed in last. "Where've you been?" she mouthed, wide-eyed with excitement.

Abby put a finger to her lips.

The next morning, she was up before the sun rose.

Although Jacob had referred to their previous success as a joint venture, Abby considered it no foregone conclusion that she would once again be permitted by Pepys to accompany Jacob on the new investigation. She had noticed that her master referred only to Standish as his "personal inquisitor", and it stung.

Abby was the one who so often provided the deductions, she knew; the sharper wit was hers. Jacob's strengths lay in his keen eye for detail - he would note things she might overlook - and in his standing, which afforded them access to people and places a mere housemaid would never reach.

Jacob was the son of the late Sir Miles Standish, former Surveyor to the Navy Board and once a friend and colleague of Mr Pepys. Both her master and her investigating partner believed Sir Miles to have been murdered, and since her fondness for Jacob had grown during their previous investigations, she hoped it was a case they would one day be permitted to pursue.

But on the morning of the 14th of September, Abigail Harcourt did not dare presume. She had risen with the dawn as usual, and silently donned her maid's clothing: skirt, bodice and apron. She tied her long, fiery red hair up, tucked it under her cotton cap, and, with a sigh, set to work cleaning out the house's cold fireplaces.

It was dark outside and the smell of the city - still smouldering after the fire - filled her nostrils.

"What on earth are you doing, girl?"

The voice made her jump. She turned to see her master, already dressed in his finest silk waistcoat and velvet doublet, topping his periwig with a feathered hat. He looked like a man who meant business.

"I beg your pardon, sir?" she said, rising and curtsying.

Pepys ushered her upstairs, towards her quarters, like a farmer herding geese. "Pack quickly, girl! You will accompany Mr Standish to breakfast, then hurry to the wherry that awaits you at the river."

She stopped. "I'm to accompany Jaco... Mr Standish to Deptford?"

"Aye, girl! Hurry!" Pepys watched her disappear up the wooden stairs and called after her. "I did witness your performance in the Brampton village hall and was mightily impressed. Were I to wish anybody to accompany my personal inquisitor on this most troubling of investigations, it would indeed be you."

On the wheeled truckle bed in her attic room lay a new set of clothing, bought for her by Pepys. Navy-blue woollen gown; a tight-fitting, boned bodice; linen petticoat; a white kerchief to drape around her neck; and an embroidered linen cap. She gasped and held her hands over her mouth. Never before had she owned an embroidered item of clothing.

Abby was aware of why her master had gone to such expense: she was representing him; dressed in such attire,

Pepys knew, men would take her more seriously. Still it felt like a promotion of sorts.

Eagerly, she tore off her stained maid's rags and dressed herself, marvelling at the quality and freshness of the material. Then, since she had no looking glass in which to admire herself, she twirled around her small floor space and imagined how fetching she must look.

Chapter Three

Deptford by Wherry

Abby and Jacob felt compelled to witness for themselves the aftermath of the fire. Having arrived at Mr Pepys's under cover of darkness, they now stood in the washed-out daylight of the early autumn morning, the devastation spreading starkly before them.

Looking south from the bottom end of Seething Lane, the wooden houses that once stood on Beer Lane and Thames Street had vanished, reduced to piles of ash. Only the stone church of All Hallows-by-the-Tower remained, as if protected by the Almighty Himself.

In silence, they walked west along Tower Street, flanked by desolation. Before them, where once stood a mass of tightly packed buildings, stretching ahead for almost two miles… nothing. Smouldering ruins, as far as the eye could see, dotted about with figures, wandering, searching through the rubble, lost.

The houses on Mincing Lane, just two streets across from Seething Lane, were gone. It became all too apparent how fortunate Pepys had been to escape the inferno.

Some small fires still burned, nearly two weeks after the conflagration had begun, and the soles of their shoes felt uncomfortably hot. Acrid smoke drifted across the scene.

Remarkably, they could make out the ancient London wall almost a mile away, up on higher ground, which had previously been obscured by the city's dwellings. Aldersgate and Cripplegate, which they had passed through on their way to Brampton, had held back the flames, but Newgate and Ludgate, furthest west, had been breached, allowing the fire to travel into Westminster.

Abigail dropped to her knees and began to weep uncontrollably. When Jacob put a hand on her shoulder, she did not look up.

"Remember what Mr Pepys said concerning the rebuilding of the city. London will return," he told her. Choking on the drifting smoke, he added, "Come, let us find our wherry."

As Abby composed herself, dusting ash off the hem of her gown, Jacob felt a tear well up and escape his right eye. It trickled down his sunken cheek, through his unshaven stubble, and he wiped it away surreptitiously before she could notice. This was his city, too.

Eventually, they would learn that 400 streets, 13,200 houses and 87 churches were destroyed in what would become known as the Great Fire of London.

Retracing their steps, they cut through Cross Lane and Harp Lane, emerging onto Water Lane, which sloped down towards the river and Custom House Quay. The Custom House itself had been destroyed by the fire, while the quay showed signs of hasty repairs, allowing river traffic to resume.

Indeed, the Thames looked busier than ever.

During the fire, the inhabitants of the city had escaped either via one of London's gates, out towards the country, or headed south towards the river. The Thames watermen, though numbered in their many thousands, had struggled to cope with the demand. The sheer weight of human traffic, their goods, the panic… It was a miracle that the reported fatalities were so low.

Now, people were returning, hoping to find some salvageable remains of their former lives.

"Mr Standish? Mr Jacob Standish?" The call came as they approached the quay.

Jacob spotted a grinning, middle-aged waterman standing in an open rowing boat, waving at him. Pushing through a throng of people, he made his way down wooden steps towards the wherry, making sure that Abby was following.

There was another waterman in the boat, who looked almost identical to the first - tweed cap, canvas coat, jutting forehead, discernible lack of chin - besides appearing decidedly grumpy.

"I am Mr Standish," said Jacob. "And this," he motioned behind him, "is Abigail Harcourt."

"I know who you are, sir. Clement Kilgore, sir, Mr Pepys's appointed Thames waterman. That, sir, is my brother, Osbert."

Osbert tutted.

"Don't you worry about him, sir," said Clement cheerily. "Finest oarsman that side of this boat."

Jacob straightened his periwig. "How, pray, did you recognise me, since we have not previously been acquainted?"

"Mr Pepys described you, sir."

"And how did he describe me?" asked Jacob, stumbling into the boat and almost toppling over the side. His hat fell off and he quickly retrieved it from the mud-brown water.

Clement looked down at Osbert, who looked up at Clement, and they chuckled in unison.

"I don't believe you wish to hear that, sir," said Osbert.

Abby, tottering in the wobbling craft, threw herself down beside Jacob before she fell, and pushed him aside to make more room. "Pay them no heed," she told him, adding in a stage whisper, "They're asses."

It was hard to tell which of the three men looked the most put-out.

As the Kilgore brothers rowed eastward down the Thames, Abby turned around and nudged Jacob to do the same. There was London Bridge, the buildings on the north end all destroyed by the fire. A gap between properties, created during a previous conflagration in 1633, had saved those further down from the flames. Just before the bridge were the smouldering ruins of Billingsgate Market and its warehouses.

They turned away at the same time, relieved beyond words to face a stretch of London untouched by the devastation.

Beyond the heavily fortified Tower of London, they passed the brewhouses and associated buildings of the large brewers, who took their water from the Thames. The river curved to the left at Wapping, a large area of reclaimed marshland, where rich merchants were building houses: extravagant ones for themselves, considerably smaller ones for their workers.

They passed Shadwell, once barely inhabited, now busy with hundreds of homes alongside shops, taverns and a private dock. Then came Ratcliff Cross, for many years the furthest point up the Thames at which large ships could offload their cargoes, since their masts were too tall to pass beneath the arches of London Bridge.

The water was murky and dotted with floating rubbish: discarded food, broken furniture, dead animals and worse. The distinct salt-smell of the incoming tidal water mingled with the decay of all that waste. London's lifeline, it may have been, but the Thames was far from picturesque.

Since the end of the Civil War, the riverside from the Tower eastwards, once so much field and bog, had become developed as merchant traders expanded their businesses. Everything that seafaring and shipbuilding folk required was now present. Beside the water were wharves, docks and the attendant tradespeople (chandlers, victualers, ropemakers, timber merchants, and so many more); behind those, houses. Behind that, green fields.

For two years, Jacob had made this journey daily. His father, Sir Miles Standish, a senior member of the Navy Board like Pepys, had used his influence to secure him the post of purser's apprentice. Jacob's academic achievements had been uninspiring; the efforts of private tutors and learned professors at Oxford had amounted to little. Rote learning held no appeal for him - Jacob preferred to learn through experience.

Not that his tenure as a purser's apprentice had been an unqualified success. On one occasion, his calculations for a frigate crew's life-saving beer ration - water being unfit to drink - had been awry by a multiple of ten. Where the

300-strong crew should have sailed with a gallon of beer per man per day, they had instead been issued less than a pint.

The error had fortunately been discovered before any harm was done, and a mutiny averted, but the vessel was forced to return to Woolwich docks. It being by no means his first miscalculation, Jacob had found himself summarily dismissed.

Abby noticed that he was frowning to himself and asked, "What troubles you, Jacob?"

He lowered his head. "My father expected me to succeed."

She knew of the failure of his brief naval career and guessed that this trip in the direction of his former workplace had triggered painful memories. "As a purser?" she asked.

Jacob nodded.

"Were you sad to lose the post?"

He shrugged. "Nay. I was never at ease among navy men."

"Wrong shape!" Clement Kilgore butted in, not breaking his rowing rhythm. "Sailors are small and wiry, aren't they? All that climbing up the rigging. You'd not get off the deck, mate. Too large."

Jacob sat up indignantly. "I served merely as the purser!"

"Failed purser," Osbert chimed in, nudging his brother.

"How dare you eavesdrop on our discourse!" said Jacob, rising angrily, then sitting straight back down again on seeing the Kilgores roll their muscled shoulders.

The boat fell silent after that.

Having navigated a long, slow bend in the river, the wherry approached Deptford Dockyard. The tide had been with them, and the Kilgore brothers, for all their faults, were skilled rowers. Jacob judged that the trip had not taken more than an hour.

The inquisitors had heard the docks before they saw them: the hammering of nails, the rasp of saws, and the shouting of labourers. In this industrialised stretch, the river was busier, and the vessels larger: barges, yachts, warships and merchantmen.

Despite the ignominy of his short-lived naval career, Jacob knew well the area and its history.

Around the next bend would be the Blackwall shipyard, he told Abby, where the all-powerful East India Company of merchant traders had once built and serviced their ships. Further downriver was the London royal dockyard at Woolwich, where he had served. Deptford was where serious shipbuilding began.

The galleons of the East India Company had led the way, large enough to carry a heavy cargo and well-armed enough to defend themselves against the most capable privateer vessels. Successive monarchs, Jacob noted, as well as the Lord Protector, Oliver Cromwell, had seen what private money could achieve, coupled with innovative, mathematical ship design, and had modified their own navy vessels accordingly.

At the present time, King Charles was engaged in the Second Dutch War, which had begun the previous year. The King wished to wrestle trade from their habitual enemy in order to achieve English dominance, but the battle would be hard-fought.

It was good news for the men of Deptford. In peace-time, the sailors were laid off without pay; Jacob had witnessed at first hand the deprivations of seafarers and their families. During wartime, these men could at least earn a living - assuming, that is, the royal purse could afford to pay them.

Deptford Dockyard had been founded by Henry VIII in 1513 and had strong associations with Britain's most famous mariners, Francis Drake - who had been knighted there by Queen Elizabeth I - and Walter Raleigh.

Abby had lived for a time with relatives in Greenwich, opposite Blackwall, and was used to seeing the vast warships and merchantmen under sail. Never, though, had her eyes beheld a dockyard from the vantage point of the river, since she could not afford a waterman's fee.

Wharves, slipways and buildings of all sizes lined the riverbank in either direction, most noticeably the two-storey, brick-built Great Storehouse with its tall

tower, which dated back to the time of Good Queen
Bess. Two huge galleons, each with three masts, lay fore-
castle-forward in the King's Ship Yard. Their flat sterns
towered above Abby and Jacob, elaborately carved and
painted in red, blue and gold.

Their wherry drifted towards its landing point at the
Upper Water Gate. Abby was already standing, ready
to disembark, before the prow of their boat thumped
lightly against a flight of wooden steps. When she looked
for Jacob, expecting to find him beside her, he was still
seated, hunched, tugging distractedly on the forelock of
his periwig.

"Come, Mr Standish," she urged him, motioning with
her hand.

"What's your business here?" enquired Clement.

"Our business is none of your business," Jacob snapped,
pleased with how it sounded.

Osbert leered at him through blackened teeth. "I'll
wager he's here to clean the privies."

Clement slapped his back, and the brothers chortled at
such wit.

"Actually, we're on the trail of a murderous plague
doctor," said Abby, stepping daintily off the boat.

Chapter Four

Henry Trevelyan

*D*uring the reign of King James I, in the fishing village of Mousehole (pronounced Mao-zel) in Cornwall, a baby boy was born to Thomas and Anne Trevelyan. They christened him Henry. It was a name fit for a king and an upstanding Anglican.

Mousehole lay in a recess of Mount's Bay, far into the south-west of England, ten miles as the crow flies short of Land's End. Although the surrounding coastline was rugged, Mousehole was sheltered from storms, and its community was deeply connected to the sea.

Thomas was a fisherman. During the lucrative pilchard season, which ran from July until November, sometimes into December, he helped net the oily fish, about the length of a man's hand, using seine nets. These hung vertically in the water, weighted at the bottom, with cork floats along the top edge. Although the seine-netting method dated back thousands of years, it served him well. On a particularly good day, one net alone could trap hundreds of thousands of fish.

The pilchards were eaten locally, as well as being salted and pressed for preservation, then exported to the Mediterranean, Italy in particular. Their oil, a by-product of the pressing, was used as fuel for heating and lighting (bearing a distinctive, fishy odour).

When the pilchard were out of season, Thomas fished for crab, lobster and crayfish, using strings of willow-woven 'withy' pots. When the weather was too rough for him to put to sea, he would weave more pots or repair his nets ashore. These traditions had been passed down from generation to generation; such was the way of the fishing community.

As little Henry grew up, wide-eyed and eager to learn, he came to view his father as a hero. It was inevitable that he would follow him to sea.

The Mousehole fishermen's cottages, constructed from local stone with slate roofs, were clustered around the harbour. This harbour, protected by an impenetrable stone wall and equipped with a wharf, provided a safe mooring place for the boats that lined up along its length.

Elsewhere, a blacksmith's forge, fish cellars for processing and storing fish, tall wooden net lofts for repairing and drying nets, and the harbour master's office served the community.

Henry's mother, Anne, was a midwife and local storyteller who filled his young head with Cornish folk tales that fired his fevered imagination.

A giant named Cormoran, she said, had built the tiny island of St Michael's Mount, which he could just make out across Mounts Bay. From there, the giant would raid the mainland for cattle to fill his rumbling stomach. He used white granite to build the island, aided by his wife, Cormelian. However, one night, when he became exhausted and fell asleep, she gathered the lighter greenstone in her apron, which was easier to find and carry. Cormoran woke, noticed her deceit, and kicked out at his wife.

The stones that fell from her apron formed Chapel Rock, Anne told her son, just offshore from St Michael's Mount.

As a small boy, Henry would gather rocks as heavy as he could carry, and stomp around the garden with them, pretending to be Cormoran. Then he would pile them high to create his own King Henry's Mount.

He believed absolutely that among the stones and hedgerows of Mousehole, piskies dwelled: little people known for their dancing, whose queen was called Joan the Wad (wad being a torch).

Likewise, the male water spirits known as Bucca were as real to him as were his mother and father. Henry would sit with his legs over the harbour wall and try to spot one of these mermen, any glint on the water's surface perhaps signalling the movement of such a creature below.

His head was alive with possibilities.

When he was eight years old, during the pilchard season of 1632, Henry was led up the steep path to a huer's hut on the headland by an old man he knew only as Peck. His father had taken him out in his boat, Anne's Hope, many times, demonstrating the various knots and fishing techniques he used. That day he was being trusted to spot the incoming shoals of pilchard - as a 'huer' - and when he did so, to cry down to the waiting boats, "Hevva!" while waving gorse bushes in his hands.

Peck, whose real name was Petroc Penhaligon, was an old man once revered for his fishing skills. Some years ago, he had broken his arm while out at sea. It had never properly healed, and he no longer had the strength to haul a net or to pull an oar, so his work became land-based. Thomas Trevelyan knew that Peck was the man to teach his son the huer's trade.

The pilchard shoals that day, chasing plankton in from warmer waters, were the largest in many a year. Guided by Peck, Henry spotted from a great distance the oil slick floating on the sea surface, which signalled the massed fish beneath it. "Hevva!" he called down excitedly to the waiting boats and the men on shore, his high-pitched, boyish voice buffeted about by the wind.

"Hevva!" called down Peck, helping him out.

It became Mousehole's record pilchard haul. In the local tavern afterwards, Henry grew tipsy on the many sips of ale offered by the celebrating villagers.

Since that day, Thomas had taken his son fishing with him whenever he went out. Young Henry learned fast. Navigation, tides, currents and reading the weather; baiting, setting and retrieving crab pots; boat, net and sail maintenance; species identification... Henry took it all in.

He was made for this life, he felt; it was in his bones. He loved leaving the land behind and heading out into that life-affirming expanse of blue-green, the boat's bow rising then crashing down as they negotiated the waves, sea spray whipping across his face and stinging his eyes. Feeling the warmth of his father as he toiled beside him, Thomas's rugged confidence almost palpable.

He cheered with joy as the fish came in with the nets, their tails flapping frantically and silver scales glinting with iridescence, knowing the catch would feed his family and the wider community for days to come. That sense of accomplishment fired his soul.

When his mother cooked fresh mackerel over a crackling fire and served them with turnip, butter and kale, he would proudly announce, "I caught those!" His father would ruffle his salt-brittle sandy hair with a huge, calloused hand, then retreat to his wooden chair by the fire and smoke a clay pipe.

But life was tough. The winters were cold, storms often battered the shore, denying the villagers their livelihoods – and there were pirates. Barbary pirates from the coast of North Africa, known as corsairs.

Working alongside privateers from Holland and even England, the corsairs raided coastal communities of countries bordering the Mediterranean and around the British Isles. Cornwall was one of their habitual hunting grounds.

Their booty was people – men, women and children, sold into the North African white-slave trade. Upwards of 60 Barbary ships would lie offshore and pounce when the fishermen headed out. They would board the fishing boats, take the men, and leave their craft drifting.

They also raided on land, dragging entire families from their homes at the point of their cutlasses. The corsairs were as feared as they were reviled.

One morning, when Henry was ten years old, his father woke early – earlier than usual, long before the sun came up – and quietly left the house without waking the boy. Henry always wondered afterwards whether his father had sensed something awry that day.

Thomas Trevelyan went out fishing, and he never came back.

As the community began their daily tasks, the Anne's Hope was spotted drifting in Mount's Bay. Henry, screaming his father's name, waded out fully clothed into the freezing water and swam to the little boat, buffeted by the currents but undaunted. When he heaved himself up over the gunwale, he knew what he would find. Young Henry wailed to the heavens and beat the timbers with his fists until they were bloodied and raw.

After that day, he became the man of the house.

Chapter Five

Theodore Penn

At close range, the yard felt even more overwhelming to Abby. The clanging and banging and sawing and yelling that rang in her ears; the smells of salt, tar and timber; the constant motion of the enormous workforce... The enormity of everything, the assault on the senses.

The massive oak gate of the dockyard was guarded by two porters. Both carried a cutlass and flintlock pistol in their belts, and were burly fellows. A steely look in their eyes suggested they enjoyed a spot of bother.

The burlier of the two stepped forward. "Halt! Who are you and what is your business here?"

Jacob took the lead. "I am Jacob Standish, and this is Abigail Harcourt. We seek entry for an urgent matter concerning the Clerk of the Acts, Mr Samuel Pepys."

The porter eyed his associate warily. "Everybody claims urgent business these days. Can you prove your affiliation with Mr Pepys?"

"I can!" replied Jacob, perhaps a little too eagerly, retrieving a sealed envelope from his satchel. After the issues with authority they had encountered in Brampton, he and Pepys had planned for just such a moment.

The porter took the envelope, inspected the wax seal, nodded to himself, and cracked it open. Having read the contents, he handed it to his colleague.

"Escort them to the Master Shipwright," the second porter ordered. "Mr Penn shall have the final word."

Abby and Jacob were led past long, narrow rectangular ponds, in which entire tree trunks, perhaps three feet in diameter and devoid of their bark, were floating.

The porter, whose suspicion of them appeared to be diminishing, anticipated Abby's question. "The mast docks. If the pine masts are not stored in water, they lose their sap and dry out."

"Much obliged to you," said Abby.

Shortly, they found themselves standing beneath the mast-less hull of a galleon they had seen from the river, sitting in a dry dock. Up close, dwarfed by the hull, it was an awe-inspiring sight.

This was a substantial warship, with three decks and dozens of gun-ports through which the cannons would fire. Enormous lengths of wood lay close by, alongside barrels of tar for waterproofing and piled, thick rope for the rigging. Men swarmed over the wooden scaffolding and timber structure like ants, hammering, sawing, painting, tarring.

So entranced by the spectacle were the inquisitors, necks craned upwards, that they did not realise their little group had been joined by a new figure.

"The Loyal London," said the newcomer, instantly gaining their attention. "One-hundred-and-twenty-seven feet long, 42-foot beam, 80 guns. A second-rate ship of the line..." He stopped and peered at Jacob. "Do I know you, sir?"

Jacob froze. He surely knew this man in the long leather apron, with the pointed nose like a raven's beak. It was Theodore Penn, Deptford's Master Shipwright, who oversaw everything at the royal dockyard, from designing the King's warships to issuing stores and policing the yard. Penn came from a long line of celebrated master shipwrights and was revered by his men.

Although he had worked for the navy downriver in Woolwich, Jacob had encountered Penn when he visited the dockyard there. He removed his hat and bowed. "Indeed, sir, I am Jacob Standish. I was once an apprentice purser at the Woolwich docks."

Penn slapped his thigh. "Jacob Standish! Who did send a frigate to war with mere thimbles of beer for the men!"

Wringing his hat in his hands, the inquisitor began stammering. "Sir... I did..."

Abby took a step forward. "Mr Penn, the Loyal London is a most magnificent ship, sir."

Penn lightly grasped the fingers of her right hand. "And who, pray tell, is this enchanting madam?"

Abby had never been referred to as "madam" before. *This outfit my master bought for me surely does the trick*, she thought to herself.

"Abigail Harcourt," she replied, adopting her most refined tone and bowing.

"Oh! How marvellous!" chirped Penn, pulling out a handkerchief and dusting his long nose.

As she withdrew her hand, Abby noticed he had spittle in the corners of his mouth.

"Sir, we are here on behalf of Mr Samuel Pepys," she said. "Concerning the grave matter of Deptford's Plague Doctor."

Penn's frivolous demeanour vanished. "You?" he said, regarding her perplexed. "Are you to investigate Deptford's murderous Plague Doctor?"

It was Jacob's turn to interject. "Sir, we serve as Mr Pepys's personal inquisitors. I hold here a letter of authorisation, duly signed by his hand."

Penn inspected the letter and handed it back. "A most extraordinary turn of events. Very well," he said. "Mr Pepys is a gentleman of unerring discernment, thus I shall trust in his judgement. No man shall hinder your passage in my dockyard. And how, pray tell, do you propose to unmask this vile miscreant and pretender to the medical arts?"

"You believe the man is no physician, sir?" Abby asked.

Penn regarded her quizzically. "A true physician is sworn to save lives, not to end them!"

Abby was about to reply when Penn continued, "Nor did I claim the Plague Doctor to be a man."

The inquisitors exchanged glances.

"I would not wish to point the finger of suspicion at any one person, however...," Penn paused for effect. "I would advise you to acquaint yourselves with the facts of the matter."

"Which are, sir?" Jacob asked.

"That Deptford Dockyard had but one plague doctor in that fearful time of pestilence, whose qualification for such great responsibility amounted to nought. The individual in question is named Lydia Mercer, a chandler by trade."

Penn explained that Mercer had lost her entire family – a husband and three sons – to the plague, shortly after it had reached Deptford in July of the previous year. Distraught and racked with guilt that she alone had survived, she became obsessed with saving others' lives. Mercer's Aid for the Afflicted was the charity she set up to help care for plague victims, using funds from her husband's successful chandlery business, which she had taken over.

Her efforts received wide approval from the broken community. Until, noted Penn, she began dressing as a plague doctor, in a uniform she had acquired for the museum she was founding. When Mercer began treating plague victims in their stricken homes – as if she had a death wish – it was agreed by most that she had become a dangerous charlatan.

"You suspect this Lydia Mercer murdered Humphrey Wilkes, sir?" asked Abby.

Jacob butted in, "A woman would not possess the strength to kill a man!"

"He was shot betwixt the eyes," Abby reminded him. "However, the Plague Doctor was seen leaving Wilkes's home. Would somebody not have noticed if it were a woman?"

The Master Shipwright disagreed, noting how the Plague Doctor's black robe concealed its wearer from head to toe – and that the figure had only ever been seen at the dead of night.

"We will surely question this Lydia Mercer," said Jacob, stroking his chin in a manner he hoped appeared wise.

"You might also question Kitty Blake," added Penn, "who is a resident of The Ship Inn."

Abby cocked her head. "You suspect this woman as well?"

The Master Shipwright nodded firmly.

"Why would that be, sir?" she asked.

Penn coughed lightly. "The woman hails from Tangier," he replied, "and there are too many tales of her shadowy past."

Chapter Six

Robert Drake

When the porter from the main gate returned to his duties there, Penn summoned a dockyard worker to escort the inquisitors to Pepys's friend, Robert Drake's house. Whether the Master Shipwright wanted them shown the way or kept an eye on, they could not decide.

Turning left and walking parallel to the Thames, they found themselves on a wide road - far wider than those in the city - lined on either side with worker's dwellings. Their escort pointed out, behind the housing on their right, a swathe of grassland which he named as Deptford Strond. Until 1618, it had been the location, he explained, for the original Trinity House, the corporation established under Henry VIII to oversee and encourage safe passage at sea. Trinity House had built their first lighthouse, illuminated by candles, in Lowestoft, Suffolk, in 1609.

Jacob was more interested in discussing the Plague Doctor than in lighthouses, and he told the fellow so. When their escort became irate, Jacob apologised, but the damage was done, and they would glean no more maritime history from the soured fellow.

Abby professed to being mystified that the Master Shipwright had named two women as his main suspects, when murder was most often committed by men. Jacob, who was more easily swayed by authority, suggested they keep an open mind.

After leaving the inquisitors outside a two-storey stone house on the southern edge of the Strond, the escort stamped off without a word. The door looked freshly painted red; beneath this new coat, Abby and Jacob could just make out the large words, 'LORD HAVE MERCY UPON HIM', and the shape of a cross. Abby shuddered at the thought of the Plague Doctor standing where she stood now, daubing on those letters.

Their investigation had become real.

A woman answered the door and introduced herself as Nora Drake, Robert's wife. When the inquisitors explained who they were, she promptly bade them enter.

Inside was warm and cosy, with padded furniture and naval-themed tapestries on the walls, and a healthy fire going. The burning logs crackled and an ornate clock, on the mantelpiece above the fireplace, ticked. The effect was immediately calming.

"Such a delightful home," noted Abby.

Nora Drake smiled. She wore a navy-blue dress with a white apron tied around her waist. Petite - roughly Abby's size - and bony, her delicate features were a far cry from the rough world outside. She looked as if she might snap in a strong wind.

"I was making coffee," Nora said. "Would you like some?"

Abby stiffened. "The drink brings back ill memories," she said quietly.

Jacob eyed her. "What ill memories, pray?"

She waved a hand dismissively. "It was nought. Master Pepys escorted me to a coffee house, where I was denied entry."

"Which coffee house?" Jacob asked.

Abby ignored him. Having first sampled tea in Brampton, the opportunity to finally taste coffee, London's most fashionable beverage, was not one she should miss. "Aye, Mistress Drake, I shall take a cup, if you please," she said.

Jacob, coming from a monied family, had visited a coffee house or two and found the drink rather unpleasant, yet affected a liking for it to appear fashionable.

As Nora poured boiling water over the roasted grounds in a tall coffee pot, then suspended that over the fire, the drink's distinctive odour began to permeate the room.

"A perquisite of Robert's work," she explained. "Living beside these raucous docks has its uses."

"Where is your husband?" Abby asked.

As she did so, the door was flung open to reveal a breathless Robert Drake.

"I heard you were here," he said, puffing. "I specifically asked Mr Pepys not to trouble you."

Nora hastened to him. "But Robert, these good people are here to assist you."

Having recovered his composure, Drake closed the door. "One of them is barely a woman, the other…" He studied Jacob's expectant face. "He's a size, for certain, however he looks half-baked."

As Jacob adjusted his periwig, Abby leapt up indignantly. "Mr Drake, we are Master Pepys's…"

Robert interjected incredulously, "You are Mr Pepys's servant?"

Abby cursed herself for referring to Pepys as her master; it was a mistake she would not make twice.

Just as the introductions reached a low ebb, Nora stepped in. "Robert, these are Mr Pepys's personal inquisitors. As you are aware, he's a man of fine judgement…"

"I know well Mr Pepys's judgement," Robert interrupted. "I consider him to be a good friend as well as a colleague, and I would not impose upon him. Already I have asked of him too many favours."

"But…" Nora began.

"But nought! I can defend myself, woman!"

Although he was noticeably short, Robert Drake, in his elegant attire with lace, velvet and frills, had an undeniably fine physique. His skin was hardened and ruddied by his life at sea, and his deep-set, dark eyes had the look of someone who embraced danger.

He glanced at the clock on the mantlepiece, which showed twenty minutes to one. "I must return to work, lest there be hell to pay," he said, turning to leave.

Nora rushed over and held him back. "Please, Robert, if not for you then for my sake, let them assist, I beg of you!"

Robert stared at Jacob then Abby: he looking childishly hopeful; she, practically petulant. He laughed and kissed his wife. "If it pleases you, my darling, then I shall allow it."

Thus, Robert tarried a short while longer. The inquisitors learned that a few days ago the Drakes had woken to find the cross and slogan daubed on their door. The same deadly warning that had been painted onto midshipman Humphrey Wilkes's door a fortnight earlier. Five days later, at midnight, Wilkes was shot between the eyes. The Plague Doctor was seen walking away.

"Are you not in fear for your life?" Jacob asked Robert.

His wife answered for him. "He is too proud to admit it. And if he genuinely is not, then I fear for him myself."

The coffee was ready, and Nora began pouring it into four stoneware cups.

Robert stopped her. "I do not wish for coffee," he said. "My time is precious."

"Then we shall conclude matters here swiftly, Mr Drake," Jacob assured him. "It is but yourself and the unfortunate Mr Wilkes upon whose doors these black crosses have been daubed?"

Drake nodded.

"Then I wonder what history you share?" Jacob asked. "Why did the Plague Doctor fix upon you both?" He caught Abby regarding him with an expression of pride. *My inquisitor's skills are improving!* he realised.

"Would you like sugar?" Nora enquired, having poured three cups.

Coffee and *sugar,* thought Abby, *in one day!* "You lead a charmed life, Mr Drake," she said.

"My husband is well-admired by the Navy Board," replied his wife, "and is well rewarded for his hard work. He received a pay rise only last month, did you not, Robert?"

Drake stared daggers at his wife. "That is my business," he told her.

"No doubt he makes more as a purser than I ever did," Jacob blurted out, immediately regretting it.

"You served as a purser?" Robert asked.

Jacob groaned quietly. "Apprentice purser."

Drake raised an eyebrow. "And now you seek out murderous plague doctors. What a curious fellow you are."

Before he left, Robert returned to Jacob's question concerning his and Humphrey Wilkes's common ground. They had both served aboard the same ships together, on voyages too numerous to mention, was all he could suggest. Other than that, he professed to be at a loss.

Nora spoke up. "If you recall also, Robert, you and Humphrey served as watchmen during the plague."

Her husband turned on her. "Once again you tell strangers my business!" he snarled, rising abruptly. "It was a dark matter which I prefer to forget, and one I surely do not wish to discuss among strangers."

With that, he was gone, slamming the door behind him.

The fire crackled, the clock ticked, and the three left behind studiously inspected their cups of coffee. Abby was finding the strange drink frankly unpalatable, although she felt obliged to finish it.

"Tell us about the watchmen," she said.

Nora hesitated only briefly before launching into the story.

As the death toll rose rapidly during the peak plague months from summer 1665 until the spring of the current year, the alderman of Deptford took drastic action, she told the inquisitors. Anyone discovered to be infected was locked in their house – with their family members – who, since they had breathed the same infected air, were considered a danger to the community. It did not matter if they were showing no ill symptoms.

Inevitably, only a very fortunate few survived. To ensure that no one attempted to escape, and to ease the suffering of those inside, watchmen were posted at their doors, one overnight and another during the day. As well as preventing the occupants from leaving, it was their duty to fetch food, water, and any other supplies requested.

As manpower was lost, businesses shut down, trading suffered, fewer ships sailed and Deptford Dockyard fell silent. Money became tight and, Nora told them, Robert was forced to accept work as a watchman, guarding over the plague houses. His partner in this was his good friend, Humphrey Wilkes.

Abby gratefully drained the last of her coffee, swallowed a slurry of grounds and began to choke. Jacob slapped her on the back while asking Nora, "Did they make enemies during that time?"

Unfortunately, he slapped her so hard that the the cup flew from Abby's hand and landed in their host's lap.

"I would not know," Nora replied, waving away his apologies with one hand, wiping coffee grounds from her apron with the other. "Robert is not a man to share his woes. However 'tis possible. The poor wretches in those houses can't have…" She trailed off, then suddenly sparked with realisation. "Nay, hold! There was somebody. They spread rumours concerning my Robert and Humphrey, that they stole from the dead and profited from such misery."

Abby, still choking on the coffee grounds, managed to gasp out, "Who was he?"

"This was no 'he'," Nora replied. "It was Lydia Mercer. Diverting suspicion, since it was she herself who stole from the dead. To fill her ghastly Plague Museum."

Chapter Seven

Confrontation

B efore they left, the inquisitors asked Nora for directions to an inn, where they could stay the night. They were also hungry. Drake's wife gave them directions to The Ship Inn, opposite the King's Shipyard, where the sailors and dockyard workers congregated after work. It was the perfect place to ask questions, she told them.

Abby and Jacob retraced their steps, discussing the case. Most startling, they agreed, was the mention, once again, of Lydia Mercer. The Master Shipwright had named her as a suspect, as now had Nora Drake. Two from two. It felt significant.

"Do you sincerely believe the Plague Doctor could be a woman?" Abby asked.

Jacob thought for a while. "I would consider it most unlikely. What woman would possess the cunning, or indeed such devilry, to resort to murder?"

"I possess such cunning," Abby replied flatly.

Before working with her, he would have scoffed at the idea. A woman, moreover, a serving girl – marked with intelligence? Unthinkable! But, of course, he had worked alongside her and had seen what she was capable of. Were he honest with himself, he found her abilities dumbfounding.

She nudged him. "What are you thinking?"

"Nought," he replied.

They had reached The King's Shipyard: the dry docks where the two painted galleons lay, which they had seen from the river. Behind that was the Great Storehouse. From this close vantage point, it looked even more vast, with one side being a covered porch with a sloping roof, where they assumed loading and offloading could be carried out in all weathers.

Nora Drake had told them to turn right when they saw the shipyard. As they did so, something caught Jacob's eye. Down at the far end of one of the dry docks, by the river… "Is that not Mr Drake?" he asked Abby.

She turned and squinted. "Aye," she said. "I believe it is."

The inquisitors watched Drake converse with another man, when a third figure, dressed in black, appeared suddenly from an alleyway on the right. Although this figure was perhaps 150 yards from them, they could make out a long robe that reached to the ground, some sort of mask entirely covering the head, with a hat… and a long, pointed beak.

"The Plague Doctor!" Abby and Jacob exclaimed in unison and began running.

Drake and his companion were facing the river with their backs to the Plague Doctor, and the men working aboard the ships were too intent on their tasks to notice.

Jacob's gangly legs being twice the length of Abby's, he was quickly well ahead of her, and her running was hampered by her long gown.

"You go ahead!" she called after him, knowing that confrontation was his domain.

Jacob sprinted forward, heart pounding, as he saw the Plague Doctor raise a flintlock pistol and take aim at Drake. At that precise moment, as if on cue in some tragic play, Drake turned.

"Mr Drake!" Jacob shouted in warning.

Horror spread across Robert Drake's face as his gaze shifted - first to Jacob, then to the Plague Doctor himself.

The Plague Doctor, startled by Jacob's cry, turned to see the inquisitor charging towards him. Panicked, he re-aimed the pistol, just as Drake ducked to avoid being shot.

Flames and smoke exploded from the pistol, and a sharp report echoed about the dock.

"Nay!" Jacob exclaimed, as Drake's companion clutched at his heart and toppled off the dockside. Distracted, the inquisitor tripped, flew through the air, crashed into a thick wooden pillar and crumpled onto the cobbles.

Despite the general commotion in the yard, a few dockworkers had heard the shot. Some began clambering down the scaffolding to investigate, while the Plague Doctor slipped away toward a cluster of buildings.

Abby, still running, found herself the closest to the assailant. That was when she felt it: fear. Abject, unadulterated fear. It ran down her spine like a chill wind and stopped her in her tracks.

"Lydia?" she called out.

The Plague Doctor stopped and turned, and in doing so, caught a boot-heel in a length of discarded chain and crashed backwards into a dockside wall. Clutching an elbow in pain, Abby's quarry continued onwards, slipping between buildings and disappearing among shadows.

A trio of dockworkers caught up with the inquisitor as she stood, hands on knees, cursing her own cowardice.

"Are you hurt?" asked one, as they gathered around her.

"Nay, I'm fine," she replied, wheezing lightly. "I'm more concerned for my companion," she told them, pointing towards Jacob's still form.

Robert Drake appeared among them. His face was white and his deep-set eyes were glazed. "He… he tried to kill me," he said. "The Plague Doctor." Then he ran off in the direction of his house.

Jacob recovered consciousness and was deemed well enough to be able to hobble, accompanied by a dockworker, to the nearby naval hospital, though blood poured from a deep, vertical gash at his hairline. By chance, his periwig had saved him from a more serious injury.

Abby had offered to accompany him, but he groggily insisted she remain, to discern all she could from the scene. Still shaken by her reaction to the confrontation with the Plague Doctor, she felt grateful for being recognised for a skill she possessed in abundance.

Walking to the riverside, she stood on the wooden embankment and peered down over the edge. The tide was low, and men knee-deep in Thames mud were attaching a harness and rope to the limp body of the Plague Doctor's hapless victim.

Others gathered around her to spectate, news of the crime having spread fast. They murmured among themselves, although the general mood did not seem as sombre as Abby would have expected.

The inquisitor watched as four dockworkers hauled on the rope until the dead man lay at her feet. His long, silver hair lay splayed on the wooden walkway, and his clothing - long silk waistcoat and a green coat with subtle gilding, suggesting a man of some standing - was drenched through. A hole in his shirt was evidence of the lead shot that had passed through him.

The dead man's face, she would never forget. His eyes stared into a void, and his mouth was agape, as if he had been confronted by a demon.

As Abby turned away from the sight, she heard a man chuckle. "Good riddance," someone else said.

"Who is he?" she asked the nearest bystander.

"That's old Joe Catchpole," came the reply. "Collector of Customs."

Someone searched through Catchpole's pockets. They retrieved a large fob watch on a chain bearing the royal coat of arms, its hands stopped at five minutes past one, and a small wooden box.

"May I see?" Abby asked.

The murmuring instantly ceased. Suddenly she, not the corpse, was the centre of attention.

She became aware of men's faces all around her, wary, peering. Beards and rotten teeth, neckerchiefs and rough skin.

"Who did you say you were?" asked the one who had identified the Customs man, his face full in hers, his breath reeking of rum.

"I work for Mr Samuel Pepys," she told him, as confidently as she could muster, taking care not to refer to Pepys as 'master'.

Instinctively, everyone in the crowd took a step backwards. Pepys visited the royal dockyard on a regular basis, in his role as Clerk of the Acts, and had the power to hire and fire.

Yet the sense of hostility lingered.

Abby added, "He has charged me with examining the Plague Doctor murders."

That stunned them briefly into silence. One man laughed, then another, and another, until Abby felt surrounded by echoing derision. Some bent double, while tears of laughter rolled down their oily cheeks. Abby could only shake her head.

"Back to work! Game's over!" came the gruff order from a voice at the back of the crowd.

As quickly as it had begun, the levity vanished. One by one, the dockworkers trooped past her, returning to their grinding daily reality.

She felt something pushed into her hand.

It was the box from Catchpole's pocket.

Opening it, she found a deck of playing cards, fortuitously saved from a soaking by the container. Fanning them out in her hand, she immediately noticed that there were two aces of spades.

Chapter Eight

The Storm

*W*ith his father gone, most likely sold into North Africa's white-slave trade, young Henry Trevelyan took the lead in the house. His mother, Anne, disappeared into a dark grief from which she never really emerged. Although she completed her daily chores admirably and remained Mousehole's most respected midwife, she stopped telling her stories and the giants went to sleep.

Her eyes became hollow and her speech slowed.

Unlike his mother, Henry packed away his sorrow and slammed the lid tight shut. His new responsibilities inspired him, and his eyes burned with righteousness. Only at night did his demons appear, as the waves crashed against the harbour wall outside, and he lay on his straw-stuffed mattress, unable to sleep.

The old fisherman, Peck, became a father figure in Thomas's absence, continuing the boy's fishing education and easing his links with the community elders. It was not always a welcome involvement. As he grew older and more confident, Henry's *impatience grew, and he showed flashes of anger. Peck, the wise old hand, knew better than to react.*

Soon Henry graduated from huer to fisherman during pilchard season, helping to row one of the seine boats and encircling the shoal in the huge net.

He grew fast and was six feet tall by the time he was thirteen, broad-shouldered and solid from his physical labours. In his oilskin coat, with a red linen kerchief of his father's wrapped around his neck, firm-jawed and green-eyed, he resembled Thomas.

When he ignored Peck's protestations and pushed his limits, putting out to sea even when a storm was forecast, his mother could only watch in anguish. Although she implored him not to go, calling him foolhardy, he brushed her aside.

"I'll fish whenever I wish," he told her. "And you'll not stop me."

Her husband, she was well aware, would never have been so reckless.

One morning, Anne found herself at the end of the pier beyond the harbour wall, staring out to sea. A blanket of coal-black clouds had turned day into night. Electric tendrils of lightning momentarily illuminated the scene before her. The waves were huge rollers, flecked with white foam, lolloping ominously as the heavens' deluge descended.

Anne's linen skirt and apron were sodden. Horizontal rain whipped into her face, stinging her skin and disguising her tears. Her son was out there somewhere, unseen.

Peck had tried to stop Henry from launching, knowing the storm was coming - Henry knew it too, but would not be dissuaded. The pair had come to blows. Eventually, Peck gave up and marched away, back to his house, cursing the boy's insanity.

"Henry!" came her desperate cry, which the gale flung back in her face. "HENRY!"

She could barely hear herself above the roar of the sea and the bedlam of the thunder. When a sudden gust of wind lifted her off her feet, almost blowing her into the boiling harbour behind, Anne Trevelyan had little choice but to abandon her vigil and return to the safety of her home.

There she found the harbourmaster, Robert Penrose, waiting for her. The most respected man in Mousehole - more so even than the alderman and parish priest - Penrose was more than the harbour administrator; he was the beating heart of the fishing community. His word was law.

Anne threw herself at his feet. "Please, Robert, save my son," she implored him.

"Your Henry's a danger to himself," he said. "If I sent men out to look for him - which I will not do - he'd be a danger to them an' all."

He took Anne by the shoulders and helped her to her feet. "Look at you, half-drowned yourself, woman. Such a pitiful state, and all the boy's fault. He ought to be ashamed."

Anne clasped her hands together and felt the sodden wrinkles on her fingertips. "Please don't blame him, Robert. He lost his father…"

The old man frowned, his leathery skin a mass of creases, "I know only too well the tale, Anne," he cut in, though speaking gently. "Thomas Trevelyan is greatly missed in Mousehole. He was a skilled fisherman and a fine husband. Would that I'd been with him the day he was taken. We'd have shown those corsairs the fight of a Cornishman." His shoulders dropped. "Yet that does not excuse your boy's…"

The door flew open with such force that it smacked into the wall behind it. In that moment, lighting struck outside, and a figure was silhouetted in the doorway, hunched and bedraggled.

"Mother," came the exhausted voice.

Anne Trevelyan fainted. The harbourmaster rushed to the door to help Henry inside.

The young man pushed him away and stared into Penrose's eyes. His right cheek was cut and swollen, and blood dripped from an angry gash across his cheek. "I need no assistance," he said.

Hobbling inside, creating puddles as he went, young Henry reached into a sodden leather pouch strapped around his shoulder. He pulled out a small, dead fish and tossed it at the harbourmaster, who let it fall to the stone floor. "The day's catch," said Henry, sneering.

The old man merely sighed.

Penrose warmed mead in a pan while mother and son, in fresh, dry clothes, sat before the fire. No one spoke. Henry's head was bowed.

The harbourmaster handed each of them a mug. "Drink," he said.

"You've no cause to seize my boat," said Henry. "Anyway, she's broken beyond mending."

"You should thank God she brought you home, Henry Trevelyan. I'd say it was a miracle," Penrose replied. "Your father built that boat…"

Henry leapt up, clutched his knee, and, crying out in pain, folded back down into his fireside seat. Instinctively, his mother went to examine the injury.

"Leave me be, woman!" he scolded her.

Penrose smacked him across his bloodied cheek. "Have some respect," he growled. "Your mother saves lives. You only endanger them."

Henry said nothing, knowing it to be true. He rose, limped heavily to the door, opened it, and walked out into the storm, watched by his mother and the old man.

"I'm away to find Peck," he said.

"You'll find no solace there, Henry," Penrose told him firmly. "Peck's had his fill of you, too."

Chapter Nine

The Ship Inn

Abby was reunited with Jacob at The Ship Inn. He was wearing a wide bandage around his forehead, which Abby thought made him look rather dashing. It also hid his overgrown eyebrows.

He had a terrible headache, he told her, but otherwise had emerged from the ordeal unharmed. He was eager to hear what she had discovered.

Three storeys high, The Ship Inn offered basic accommodation on the top floor and victuals on the other two. The ground floor, the inquisitors discovered, was the raucous one. As Abby entered, spying Jacob at a table by the fireplace, already tucking into a beef pottage, a fight broke out between two sailors. The other patrons - and there were many, it being around dinner time - crowded around the brawlers, chanting, stamping their feet, egging on one or other combatant.

The fight was broken up not by the burly man behind the counter, whom Abby took to be the innkeeper, but by an exotic-looking woman in her mid-thirties, with skin the colour of amber.

The instant she appeared in the centre of the throng, as if from nowhere, the crowd parted and returned to their tables. The drunken brawlers dusted themselves down and apologised. One lunged at the woman for a kiss; she delicately sidestepped and he fell to the floor, causing much merriment and jeering.

As ethereally as she had appeared, she was gone.

"I wager that was Kitty Blake," Jacob told Abby, referring to The Ship's resident, whom the Master Shipwright had thrown suspicion upon. "She resembles no murderer to me."

"Mr Standish, are you besotted?" she teased.

He spluttered, failing to find the words.

Abby reached across the table and took some of Jacob's bread. "Fear not, I merely jested," she said through a mouthful, then, swallowing, added pensively, "But 'tis clear she casts a spell over men."

"You believe she could enchant a man to murder on her behalf?"

"Only the fool speculates, Jacob."

Abby, having outlined her findings at the dockside to Jacob, showed him the boxed deck of cards retrieved from Joseph Catchpole's pocket. He fanned them out across the table and noticed the same thing she had: two ace-of-spades cards.

"A cheat's deck," he said.

When he turned the cards over, he saw that they were all branded with the name of an inn: The Ship Inn. As one, they stared at the innkeeper.

"You think he allows gambling?" asked Jacob.

"Come," said Abby, making for the counter. "I'm starving."

The innkeeper introduced himself jovially enough as Arthur Hall. He wore a white shirt with billowing sleeves and a long brown waistcoat. Behind him were stacked barrels, wooden shelving and a half-open door, through which the inquisitors could smell roasting meats and fish.

The spacious tap-room reeked of men: old muskets hung on the walls amid sea-faring paraphernalia, while the ceiling was stained dark brown by tobacco smoke. Every single patron seemed to be smoking a pipe.

Hall was powerfully built with a square head, crooked nose and fists the size of cannonballs. Though in his late forties, he looked more than capable of holding his own. "What brings you to my hostelry?" he asked, his voice low and gravelly.

When Jacob told him, what little charm he had feigned evaporated.

"You'll get victuals and board from me, and nought else," Hall told them. "We don't encourage," he spat out the word, "*inquisitors* at The Ship."

Abby pushed the deck of cards across the counter towards him. "Do you recognise these?"

Hall swept them off the surface with a giant hand and put his face in Abby's. "Nay, I do not," he replied, his tone suggesting an end to the matter.

At such close range, she could make out the pits in his skin; a hollowness in his chestnut-coloured eyes spoke of a darkness in his soul. "I'll have the beef pottage," she said.

Hall belly-laughed. "A wench with spirit! I admire that!" He poked Jacob in the chest, causing the inquisitor to start. "You, sir!"

Jacob did his best to look unperturbed. "Aye?"

"Would you fight me?"

"For what reason?"

"For no reason whatsoever!"

"Then I would not, sir."

"Aye," said Hall, pouring ale from a barrel for them. "I thought as much."

"The man should be in Bedlam!" Jacob hissed to Abby.

Abby, relieving her dry throat with Hall's ale, nodded. She had picked up all the playing cards from the floor and placed them in her satchel.

Jacob leaned in close to her and whispered, "Might Hall be the Plague Doctor?"

"I don't think so," she replied. "He seems too large. But I couldn't be certain. Everything happened so quickly, and the Plague Doctor's cloak disguises so much of his shape." She gulped down more ale, before adding, "Our assailant looked to be more of a regular build."

"Then I suggest…" Jacob stopped mid-reply, noticing that the inn had fallen silent.

Kitty Blake had returned. She was seated on a tall stool in a far corner of the tap-room, holding an instrument resembling a lute. All eyes were on her.

Illuminated by a pair of wall lanterns, her skin glowed, and polished metal discs on her brightly coloured silken robe intermittently caught the light, glinting like stars. She wore a vibrantly embroidered headscarf.

As Kitty fingered her instrument's short neck, set with shimmering abalone mother of pearl, the patrons cheered. Jacob noticed Arthur Hall resting his elbow on his counter and his chin on his huge fist, clearly smitten.

How alluring she was!

"This is 'The Coasts of High Barbary'," Kitty announced. Accompanied by her strumming, she began to sing.

Look ahead, look astern,
Look the weather in the lee.

Blow high! Blow low! And so sailed we!
I see a wreck to the windward,
And a lofty ship to lee.
A-sailing down all on,
The coasts of High Barbary.

Oh are you a pirate?
Or a man-o-war? cried we.
Blow high! Blow low! And so sailed we!
O no! I'm not a pirate!
But a man-o-war, cried he.
A-sailing down all on,
The coasts of High Barbary.

For broadside, for broadside,
They fought all on the main.
Blow high! Blow low! And so sailed we!
Until at last the frigate,
Shot the pirate's mast away.
A-sailing down all on,
The coasts of High Barbary.

With cutlass and gun,
O we fought for hours three.
Blow high! Blow low! And so sailed we!
The ship it was their coffin,
And their grave it was the sea.

A-sailing down all on,
The coasts of High Barbary.

All present joined in with the chorus of *"Blow high! Blow low! And so sailed we!"* By the final two verses, the inquisitors found themselves doing the same, such was the bravado of Kitty Blake's performance.

After a dozen more songs, some high-spirited, others melancholy - telling of love lost and lives damned at sea - she put down her instrument and began walking across the litter-strewn wooden floor.

Jacob kicked Abby under the table. "She comes this way!" he hissed.

By the time Abby, who had been studying something floating in her ale, looked up, Kitty was taking a seat next to Jacob. His expression had frozen into a rictus grin.

The delicate scent of rosewater wafted across the table.

"Kitty Blake," she said, extending a hand for Jacob to kiss.

When he did not move, she retracted it, puzzled.

"Is your companion unwell?" Kitty asked Abby.

"He received a blow to the head," Abby replied, nodding towards Jacob's bandage. "However I can't help noticing you have a curious effect upon men."

Kitty smiled demurely and lowered her head.

Aye, you know it, thought Abby.

"From where do you hail?" Jacob managed to ask, finally freed from his trance.

"From Tangier, in Morocco," she replied, fixing his gaze.

"You're a long way from home," said Abby.

Not taking her deep-brown eyes off Jacob, she asked him, "Will you buy me a drink?"

Kitty's drink of choice was rum, a spirit to which the locals were not unaccustomed. As Jacob well knew from his experience as an apprentice purser, every man aboard a navy vessel was allocated a rum ration. Having drunk the spirit himself, he had often wondered how they managed to sail straight.

Her real name was Katharina Al-Yazid, Kitty told them. Her family in Tangier had been market traders, selling all manner of wares that came into the city on ships from Portugal and Spain. She had been the family's go-between, mastering both languages and building up a network of contacts. When the English took over the port in 1661, it meant another tongue to learn.

"And most excellently you did learn it," said Jacob, twirling a strand of his periwig. With that, he snapped to his feet and trotted off to the counter like a well-trained King Charles Spaniel.

"When did you come to England?" Abby asked.

"Two years ago," she replied, then laughed, revealing teeth whiter than any the inquisitor had ever seen. "I fell in love with a handsome English sea captain, who stowed me aboard his ship. Now I'm here, earning my living through song."

Abby finished her drink. She was starting to feel a bit light-headed. "Where is the English sea captain now?"

"I had hoped you would tell me, as Samuel Pepys's inquisitors."

Abby looked at her quizzically. "How would we know…?"

Kitty held her finger against Abby's lips. "Let us not talk of handsome English sea captains."

Jacob returned to the table with two more ales and another rum. "I do believe the innkeeper is taking a liking to me," he said.

"He takes a liking to your money," Kitty replied, patting Jacob's stool for him to sit on. "You should be wary here. The navy does not pay its men, so they are becoming desperate."

"*Not pay them?*" Abby noticed she was slurring.

"The King has no money," Kitty shrugged. "That is what I was told. So his navy goes unpaid and Arthur's takings are down."

Emboldened by the ale, Abby broached the subject of their investigation. "Do you know of the Plague Doctor?"

"Everybody knows of him," the singer replied. "Why do you ask me?"

"The Master Shipwright believes you are involved."

A fleeting scowl marred Kitty's silk-smooth features, and was gone. She smiled and looked around the room, alighting upon Arthur Hall. "Theodore Penn would be better served directing his suspicions elsewhere," she said. "Our host, for instance. Did you know that he was once a sailor?" When the inquisitors shook their heads, she went on, "He worked for the East India Company, sailing the Indian Ocean, bringing back gold, silver and rare spices.

"He began stealing cargo and selling it on the black market. When he was discovered, some say he killed a man. For many years, he rotted in jail."

"He's a dangerous man, that much is apparent," said Abby. "Is there good reason he would murder Humphrey Wilkes and make an attempt on Robert Drake's life?"

Kitty pursed her lips. When Drake and Wilkes were watchmen during the plague, she told the inquisitors, a quarrel had developed, concerning the requisitioning of Hall's family's land as a plague pit for the dead victims.

Hall would not give up the land, she said, claiming corruption at high levels, and a violent scuffle broke out. Drake and Wilkes attacked the innkeeper with their swords, and Drake stabbed him through the side.

"Then I doubt we will see either man in this inn," said Jacob.

"On the contrary," Kitty replied. "They are here often."

"He has forgiven them?" asked Jacob, raising an eyebrow.

"Never! But their money is good."

Abby tapped the table rather drunkenly. "A fine tale!" she said. "Now I wonder, Katherina Al-Yazid, is there also good reason *you* might wish the same men dead?"

The women glared at one another.

Jacob, who was also now feeling rather bleary, failed to notice the stand-off. "Is it true?" he asked. "Drake stabbed Hall?"

Kitty flashed her teeth. "Why don't you ask him?"

Jacob made to rise, but she pulled him back down and motioned towards the burly innkeeper, who was wiping a tankard with a grimy cloth. "I told you to be wary. He hides a weapon in an oak box behind the counter and is not afraid to use it."

Abby straightened. "A flintlock pistol, such as the Plague Doctor uses?"

Chapter Ten

Wilkes's Widow

A bby woke much later than was her custom, a clump of her red hair plastered to her cheek. Her mouth was parched and she had to pry open her left eyelid. *What was I thinking?* she wondered.

Rising too quickly, her head pounded. She sat on the side of her rickety wooden bed and groaned to herself. The contents of her satchel lay scattered across the floor. The book she made case notes in was lying open, and her quill and ink bottle were near the door. Searching for her spare hair ribbon, she found it under the bed, beside the two halfpennies she kept for emergencies.

As Abby replaced the items in her satchel, she re-alised: Catchpole's box and playing cards… They were missing.

Although they were hungry, the inquisitors decided to forego breakfast at The Ship. Arthur Hall was up and about - "Fine morning!" he hailed them, grinning at their dishevelment – and neither relished a confrontation. Kitty Blake was nowhere to be seen.

The dockyard clamour engulfed them as they emerged into Deptford's tainted salt air. Abby covered her ears with her hands. She had already told Jacob about the missing – stolen – cards and they both knew who to suspect.

"Where to?" he asked.

"Lydia Mercer or Humphrey Wilkes's widow?"

Nora Drake had given them directions to both, which Abby had written down.

Incapable of making a decision with such a hangover, Jacob pulled a silver shilling from his pocket and flicked it into the air. "Heads, Lydia," he said. "Tails, Wilkes's widow."

Following Upper Watergate to King Street, they turned left onto Butcher Row, then continued past a row of workers' accommodation parallel to the river. The houses were poorer here, weather-beaten and in varying states of disrepair. The nearby river smelled foul.

"There," said Jacob, pointing towards one of the crooked wooden doors.

Abby then saw them too, daubed on the bare wood: the black cross and those words they had come to fear.

'LORD HAVE MERCY UPON HIM'.

Wilkes's widow had not painted over it.

As the inquisitors hovered there, solemnly inspecting the words, a baby's wails came from within. Abby bit her lower lip as she knocked on the door.

A young woman opened the door to them with a child, less than a year old, clutched at her chest. Its face was grimy and wet with tears. She had wrapped it in a rough grey woollen blanket and she looked exhausted.

Her long brown hair was knotted and matted, and her eyes were dull and sunken. She wore a long woollen dress, ripped at the back, and her once-white apron was covered in grime.

When the baby set eyes on Abby, it ceased howling and gazed at her intently. Instinctively, she held her hands out to take the child. The mother hesitated.

"Please," said Abby. "Let me assist."

Maggie Wilkes lived with her infant daughter, Emma, in a single-room house provided by the Navy Board. The house's dilapidated exterior gave little hint of the charm within. The walls were adorned with a few watercolour paintings of sea battles and charcoal sketches of Maggie alongside a man the inquisitors assumed to be her late husband. The drawings depicted a stocky fellow with an eye-patch over his left eye and a wry, rakish smile.

The furniture – a bed, table and chairs – was made from sturdy oak and the seats were all upholstered. It would have been a cosy space, had the central fireplace not lain cold. Above them, wooden beams and the empty roof space only added to the sense of chill.

"Why do you not light the fire?" Jacob asked.

Maggie pulled two chairs out, so that they could sit around the table. When she was satisfied with the arrangement, she told him, "The chimney's blocked; I'm awaiting the sweep."

At the table, Abby asked what Maggie recollected of the night of the Plague Doctor's visit.

Baby Emma having fallen asleep in Abby's arms, the inquisitor handed the child back. Clutching her daughter tightly to her chest, Maggie began rocking back and forth. "I was returning from my sister's with Emma when I saw him," she said, her voice timid and hesitant.

"You saw him yourself?" Jacob asked. "The Plague Doctor?"

She nodded. "I didn't know what to think. We hadn't seen a plague doctor in months."

"He came from your house?" asked Abby.

"Nay... Well, aye, but I wasn't aware of it at the time. He was on the street you've just walked, and could have come from any of the houses. That is why I didn't confront him. I had no idea what he had just done." Her face crumpled.

Abby leaned across and rubbed her arm soothingly. "Please, continue."

Maggie looked at her sleeping baby. "He walked past me," she said quietly.

"Did he speak?" asked Jacob.

She shook her head. "Though I wished him a good night."

Abby turned to Jacob. "Was he concerned she might recognised his voice?" Then to Maggie, she asked, "Did you observe anything out of the ordinary about him?"

"Besides his attire? Nay, I do not…" She paused. "There was one thing. He stepped heavily, as if with a limp."

Abby glanced at Jacob. "I glimpsed him running only briefly, and I was panicked, but I'd swear the Plague Doctor I saw yesterday had no limp."

"Perhaps he was injured and has since recovered?" Jacob suggested. He turned to Maggie and asked, "Then you returned here to find your husband brutally slain?"

Abby scowled at him as Maggie burst into tears, which woke little Emma up, who began to howl.

When calm was eventually restored, Wilkes's widow recalled in a breaking voice how she had discovered her husband lying dead on their bed. Her screams had woken the neighbours.

"Who might wish your husband dead?" Abby asked.

"Fie!" she exclaimed, a first spark of life coming to her face. "You aren't familiar with the rivalries of a dockyard?"

Jacob grimaced. "I surely am," he replied, from bitter experience. "Well do I recall…"

Maggie interjected, "There are two despicable men, by the names of Alfred Bradshaw and Hugo Hedges. Bradshaw is a merchant here in Deptford; Hedges operates a warehouse on the wharf. That pair and my husband served together aboard the King's ships many a time, and they hated each other."

There was one particular event, however, she said…

Hedges had been the carpenter's mate and Bradshaw the bosun, on a sailing to Tangier the previous year. On the return journey to England, a mutiny brewed over the shocking conditions and lack of pay.

The captain came to hear of it and wished to seek out and punish the ringleaders. Her husband swore that Bradshaw and Hedges were the culprits, but they, in turn, blamed Wilkes. As an able seaman of lower rank than the other two, his pleas of innocence appeared hopeless. Until, out of the blue, the captain sided with her husband.

"Why the sudden change?" asked Abby.

"Humphrey did not say."

Following a court martial aboard ship, Maggie went on, Bradshaw and Hedges were found guilty, although a lack of solid evidence meant they escaped capital punishment and were handed a flogging - 36 lashes each before the assembled crew, swearing they would avenge the humiliation. The resentment between the two parties festered afterwards and refused to diminish.

"Ere he was so brutally slain, Humphrey told me he had grown wary of certain of his crew-mates. Something transpired between them, which he would not divulge to me. Yet he was always at loggerheads with Bradshaw and Hedges," Maggie concluded.

"Might one of them be the Plague Doctor?" Abby asked.

"That is my belief. It was dark when I saw the fiend, and the garb hides its wearer. It could have been either of them; they have a similar stature. But mark my words, it was one of them."

As they prepared to depart, Jacob handed Maggie the silver shilling he had tossed earlier. Despite the inquisitors' protestations, she refused to accept it, repeating, "I ask for no charity."

"Does the navy not recompense you for the loss of your husband?" Abby asked.

She stormed to a bag hanging by a nail from a wall, pulled out a fistful of identically printed pieces of paper, and shook them angrily. "This," she raged, "is how the navy pays me!"

Abby looked confused.

"Tickets," explained Jacob. "Issued in lieu of pay, which may be exchanged for money at the Navy Office, whenever the King can afford to pay. As Kitty Blake told us yesterday, he cannot."

Maggie laughed bitterly. "Or I may sell them to some black-market hag at the docks, who keeps a king's ransom for herself. My husband knew all the underhand brokers of Deptford, whom he could trust to give a fair return. For my part, I know nought of them."

Baby Emma started to cry again.

Chapter Eleven

Lydia Mercer

A passing dockworker told them how to find Lydia Mercer's chandlery, on the eastern edge of the dockyard. "Beside the market," he told them. The prospect of refreshment quickened their pace, the tension at Maggie Wilkes's house having only made their hangovers worse.

Passing the Drakes's - Jacob knocked but no one answered - they turned right at the end of Deptford Strond and found themselves on the Common Green, heading towards a towered building they discovered to be St Nicholas Church.

Stretching ahead were green fields with stone and hedge boundaries. Each had been put to a different use: on some grew orchards; on others, crops and vegetables; elsewhere, sheep and cows grazed. Trees lined the dirt road that led out towards the county of Kent.

At last, the inquisitors heard the ringing cries of market traders. Rounding a corner, they found a bustling market square encircled by shops. So thirsty were they that they both broke into a trot.

Jacob overtook Abby. Turning to tease her, he tripped over his heel and fell backwards into a fruit cart. While he dealt with the irate owner, she skipped past him, making for the baker's stall and its tantalising aroma of freshly baked bread and pies.

She was chewing gratefully on a meat pie when he caught up, cradling fruit in his arms.

"What are those?" she asked.

"Bruised apples and pears," he replied. "The fearsome wench obliged me to purchase them."

Abby grabbed a pear and tore into its flesh, seeking the sweet juice. "Thank heavens for your clumsiness," she told him, beaming.

As they ate, they cast their eyes around the shops and office buildings that bounded the market square. Apothecary, butcher, tailor, cobbler, fishmonger... "There," said Jacob, pointing.

The wide, two-storey timber building's sign read: 'Mercer & Sons, Chandlery'. Through the shopfront's large, latticed windows, they could make out assorted seafaring paraphernalia.

Brushing crumbs off the front of her dress, Abby asked Jacob, "Since a life among seafarers didn't suit you, what did you hope to become?"

His jaw halted mid-bite and he stared at her, flummoxed. Never before had he been asked such a personal question, least of all by a woman. What did he *hope* to become? He did as his father told him - or at least, he endeavoured to - and that was the end of the matter.

When he told her so, she smiled.

"Why do you smile?" he asked.

"You consider yourself hard done by, Mr Standish."

"I do not!" he replied, more high-pitched than he had intended. "My father's wishes for my future mirrored my own, as is only right and proper."

Abby started on another pear, since they had plenty. "What of my father's wishes for my future?" she asked coyly.

"What of them?" Jacob was aware that Abby's father, Ambrose, a printer, had taught her to read and write at an early age. "You are a woman, after all."

She raised an eyebrow. "He hoped that I might avoid a life of service."

"Which you have!"

Abby looked down at the clothing Mr Pepys had bought her. "You refer to this?" she asked. "A theatrical disguise, so that I may fulfil a role?"

"You are Mr Pepys's inquisitor," Jacob persisted.

"Nay, Mr Standish. You're his inquisitor. I remain his housemaid in all but appearance."

Jacob scowled. "I suggest you learn some gratitude." He stormed off towards Mercer & Sons.

Abby watched him go, a flicker of amusement crossing her face.

She caught up with him at the door of the chandlery. Gulls were squawking overhead, and children darted among shoppers, squealing delightedly. Jacob looked down at Abby, who was half his size, touched her gently on the shoulder, and walked inside.

Shelves lined the walls, displaying an array of meticulously arranged wares: bolts of canvas, candles, lamp oil, tar, pitch, ropes, nails, hooks... All manner of items for the seafaring community, a selection of whom were inside, browsing. A pleasing scent of wax and wood permeated the air.

A wooden counter ran the length of the back wall, from which hung chains, rope and further shelving. Behind it was a boy, aged ten or eleven, weighing nails, alongside a tall, angular woman with a shock of ginger hair, who appeared to be in charge. In front of the counter, a finely attired man was unloading a crate of pots and pans for her inspection.

The inquisitors suddenly realised that all three had stopped what they were doing and were staring at them.

"Good day," said Jacob, bowing lightly. "I am..."

"I know who you are," the woman interrupted. "Word travels quickly around Deptford."

"Aye," said the man. "I also."

Abby ignored him and addressed the woman. "You're Lydia Mercer?"

She studied Abby and Jacob with suspicion. "Aye, I'm she. So this is whom the great Samuel Pepys sends to unmask the notorious Plague Doctor?"

Having previously discounted the idea that the murderer might be a woman, it struck Abby now that Lydia was roughly the same height as the masked figure she had seen. Although the chandler was only in her late thirties, Abby guessed, her lined, drained face suggested someone ten years older. Her clothing – long black dress and white apron – was plain, and she wore a gold ring on each of her fingers.

Lydia noticed Abby eyeing the rings. "My Richard hated jewellery," she told her. "Not much he can do about it now." She paused. "Here to dredge up the past, are you?"

"Where were you yesterday at one of the clock?" Jacob asked. "When Joseph Catchpole met his untimely end?"

The chandler burst into a disturbing cackle. "That boorish oaf! He had it coming!"

"You didn't like him?" Abby asked.

"He didn't like me! Forever scheming to have my trading licence revoked, the damned tyrant knave."

Jacob grabbed her by the wrist. "Would you commit murder? Are you the Plague Doctor?"

Lydia stared at him mockingly. "Aye. What if I am? Will you prove it, amateur inquisitor?" She tugged on his periwig. "With this sorry mane that looks plucked from a privy?"

Jacob took a step back, instinctively adjusting the hairpiece.

"May I introduce the charmer, Lydia Mercer?" the man beside them quipped, chuckling.

Snapping her head towards him, Lydia slammed her palms on the counter, causing the serving boy to flinch. "I saved this town from the plague, Hugo Hedges, and don't you forget that!"

"Many would disagree," he replied calmly.

"You're Hugo Hedges?" Abby asked him.

He looked down at himself as if checking. "It does appear so!"

Here, by good fortune, was the warehouse owner and former naval carpenter, suspected by Maggie Wilkes of being the Plague Doctor. Abby sized him up and, again, could not readily discount the possibility.

He wore a black velvet doublet with gold stitching and a wide-brimmed, feathered hat. Long, brown hair curled over his shoulders, and his ingratiating smile might have dazzled, had not the colour of his teeth matched that of the doublet.

Hedges bowed obsequiously.

By the time he was upright again, Lydia Mercer had leapfrogged the counter and was in his face. "I saved those people's lives!" she snarled.

Jacob prised them apart. "Pray, let us have no fisticuffs!"

Customers stopped what they were doing to watch the scene unfold. One or two left in disgust at such an unseemly display.

Hedges, who appeared to find the confrontation amusing, taunted the chandler. "Tell that to the poor souls who died. Or to the ones you maimed, false doctor."

Jacob took charge of the escalating situation. Pointing at the door behind the counter, he addressed the serving boy. "That door," he said. "Where does it lead?"

"Through storerooms to Mistress Mercer's living quarters, sir," the lad replied.

"Good. I shall escort Mistress Mercer there. Abby, see Mr Hedges out." Jacob turned back to the boy. "Can you look after the shop for a few minutes?"

The lad nodded.

But Hedges was already on his way out, dragging his empty crate. "I can see myself out," he called back. "I'll return for my fee on the morrow!"

"Pompous swill-belly!" Lydia shouted after him, struggling to free herself from Jacob's grasp.

The three of them negotiated a long, ill-lit corridor with doors on either side and another, barely visible amid the gloom, at the far end. Jacob found himself bouncing off the walls as he tried to control the wriggling, cursing chandler.

Abby opened the end door to reveal a spacious room, its fireplace cold, empty besides a table, two stools and an easel. Two large leaded glass windows and a row of wall lanterns illuminated the space. The inquisitors found themselves rooted to the spot, mouths agape.

The walls were covered, floor to ceiling, with notices from the days of the plague, and paintings. Paintings of the same man and three boys, some finished, some rough, in oils, watercolour and charcoal. In some, the subjects smiled happily; in others, painted in red and black, features crazily distorted, they howled in anguish.

"My favourite boys!" Lydia announced.

Being surrounded by the images of her late family seemed to placate Lydia. While Abby sat beside her, making calming talk, Jacob took the opportunity to walk around the makeshift gallery, taking it all in.

A page torn from a book showed an illustration of two surgeons and a cadaver, titled 'The Manner of Dissecting the Pestilential Body'.

The cover of a pamphlet, printed by John Bill and Christopher Barker, Printers to the King in 1665, read:

"Certain necessary DIRECTIONS As well For the Cure of the PLAGUE, As for preventing the INFECTION with Many easy Medicines of small Charge very profitable to His Majesties Subjects. Set down by the College of Physicians."

A single-page LONDON GAZETTE, dated Monday September 3rd to Monday September 10th, 1666, concerning the "lamentable accident of Fire lately happened", noted, "Diverse strangers, Dutch and French were, during the fire, apprehended, upon suspicion that they contributed mischievously to it, who are all imprisoned…"

Weekly Bills of Mortality, which cost one penny, were pasted randomly around the room. Instigated by London's parish leaders, these bills recorded the causes of death of citizens on a weekly basis. They were compiled by searchers, who were generally old women with no medical training whatsoever.

Jacob came across a Bill of Mortality dated 19th-26th September, 1665, the week in which plague deaths had peaked, recorded there as numbering 7165 in that one week. It chilled the young inquisitor's blood. How fortunate he had been, it struck him, to have lived through that dreadful time.

Elsewhere on the same bill, he saw:

Aged: 43

Burnt in his Bed by a Candle at St Giles : 1
Consumption: 134
Cough: 2
Frighted: 3
Grief: 3
Killed by a fall from the Belfry at All Hallows: 1
Lethargy: 1
Stillborn: 17
Wind: 3

Those recent horrors of fire and plague, so easily forgotten during the inquisitors' whirlwind investigations, came flooding back.

Equally disturbing were the portraits and pictures of Lydia's husband and sons. Abby coaxed their names from the still-grieving widow: husband, Richard, and sons, Christopher, Joseph and Daniel, aged 38, 20, 19 and 11, respectively.

Lydia, being a talented artist, had captured so much emotion in each of her loved ones' expressions, that it was heartbreaking to witness. The hope in young Daniel's eyes; the pain in her husband's as he gazed in anguish, hands outstretched, at three lifeless forms covered with blankets in their beds. In some paintings, the faces were eerily lifelike; in others, the skin cracked and fell away, exposing bright-white bones behind.

The easel in the centre of the room had a painting on it, which was covered in a large cloth. When Jacob went to peek underneath, Lydia was off her stool in a flash. "How dare you!" she shrieked, hammering at his chest with her fists. "My paintings are my mind writ large! They are personal, until I choose to reveal them!"

The inquisitor backed off, palms raised in apology.

Placated, Lydia returned to her stool and began her story.

Her eldest son, Christopher, worked in the grain store, she said. He fell to the plague first, in July 1665. He had taken to his bed complaining of fever and nausea, and a single, cruel week later, he was dead. When her other sons began showing similar symptoms, she and Richard had nursed them day and night.

The navy's physician in Deptford was away at sea, so their only professional support came from the local surgeon - who proved to be a barely trained man spouting quack theories. The frantic situation became only worse when Lydia discovered a red cross daubed on their door and the slogan 'LORD HAVE MERCY UPON US'. They were to be quarantined together.

"The watchmen outside our house were Humphrey Wilkes and Robert Drake," she said.

"Did you grow to despise them?" Abby asked.

"Though we beat upon our locked door and pleaded to be set free, they would not listen," Lydia replied, then sighed deeply. "Yet we are creatures driven by necessity."

Her middle son, Joseph, died next, she recalled. Then her youngest son began exhibiting symptoms, and a week later he too died. "Little Daniel fought the hardest of all my brave boys. My Robert died last, of the plague or of a broken heart, it is of no concern now."

Forty days later, Robert Drake unlocked the door and she was allowed outside. She had been spared. How and why, she could not comprehend.

Afterwards, driven by grief and zeal, she vowed to save as many lives as she could, so that others might be spared the torment she had been forced to endure.

Funded by the successful chandlery business, Lydia explained that she threw herself into medical research, buying books and equipment, and stocking her shelves with herbs and salves from the local apothecary. She corresponded with physicians, volunteered at pest houses where plague victims were treated, even attended dissections disguised as a gentleman (since women were not admitted). By some miracle, the pestilence never touched her.

Lydia's charity, Mercer's Aid for the Afflicted, provided food and medical supplies for poor families in Deptford, whose doors, like her family's, had been sealed. Recognising that future generations could learn from her work, she also founded Deptford's Plague Museum, on the waterfront.

That was when the rumours began circulating, accusing her of stealing from plague victims' homes, purloining exhibits for her museum.

"Did Wilkes and Drake start the rumours?" Jacob asked. "That is what we were told by…"

"Hush, Jacob!" Abby cut in.

The chandler laughed. "I can imagine who told you. Maggie Wilkes! She hates me, and 'tis mutual. If it were those two who started the rumours, 'tis as likely they were covering for their own crimes. I stole nothing," she asserted. "I possessed only goodness and hope in my heart during those terrible days. I saved lives."

Initially, she said, the Deptford community supported her efforts. However, as the death toll rose and her methods proved fruitless, they turned against her. With shipbuilding in abeyance and the dockyard businesses already struggling, many of her customers switched to a rival chandlery.

Increasingly desperate to make some meaningful progress, Lydia purchased a plague-doctor outfit and began treating the sick. She dared not speak, since her voice would reveal her to be a woman.

One night, she attended the home of a delirious naval officer suspected of having the plague. She was dubious about the diagnosis, she told the inquisitors, and instead suspected a foreign fever. A quack surgeon, also present, insisted the officer had developed gangrene of the hand from an infected bubo and performed an amputation. Briefly lucid and raging, the officer wrenched the mask from Lydia's head, and she was discovered.

Word spread, Lydia told the inquisitors; from being merely distrusted, she became reviled. People would spit on her in the street and threaten her. Forced to spend several weeks in hiding, she emerged only after the plague had abated and life had returned more or less to normal. Still, many in Deptford avoided her, and dark memories lingered. "My business clings to solvency by a thread," she said.

Her tale done, Lydia lay her head on the table. Resting her left cheek on her hand, she closed her right eye, as if she were going to sleep.

Jacob noticed that she was staring at him through the other eye.

Unsettled, he told Abby, "We should go."

"Do you still possess your plague-doctor garb?" Abby asked Lydia.

Lydia slowly rose and walked to an oil portrait of her husband. It depicted Richard Mercer in velvet and silk finery, clutching a scroll. "Why do you ask?" she enquired.

Abby said nothing.

Running her index finger along her husband's smiling lips, Lydia leaned in and lightly kissed the painting. After a long pause, she replied, "Aye. 'Tis in my Plague Museum."

Chapter Twelve

Escape

Seventeen-year-old Henry Trevelyan didn't take kindly to being reprimanded by Robert Penrose. Mousehole's harbourmaster, Penrose may have been, yet Henry recalled his father having little time for the old man. "He won't take risks," Thomas would tell his son.

Henry keenly recalled the oft-related tale of the Sea Star. The yawl had been spotted in trouble outside Mounts Bay during a storm of March 1630. While Penrose counselled against a rescue, several fishermen professed their willingness to try.

Against Penrose's orders, Thomas leapt into his boat, Anne's Hope, and set out towards the flailing mast of the Sea Star. He was accompanied by his friend, the seasoned fisherman, William Tregarth. So the story went, Thomas's parting words, carried on a howling wind, were: "I've faced worse seas than this!"

During the daring rescue, the Mousehole men managed to bring their boat alongside the Sea Star. Desperately lashing the craft together amid the turmoil, Thomas and William managed to drag the exhausted, three-strong crew aboard the Anne's Hope. Tragically, as they were about to depart, a massive wave crashed over them, breaking the yawl's mast. As it fell, it knocked Tregarth unconscious; he toppled into the sea and was lost in a dreadful moment.

Although he was only six at the time, Henry cursed himself for missing the dramatic events, which divided the close-knit community. Certain villagers would leave a room when Thomas entered, unable to reconcile their feelings. One of them was Robert Penrose.

Henry noticed the hostility, even at that young age, and questioned his father about it. "Not everyone agrees with the choices we made that day," Thomas told him. "Some believe it was reckless, and the price we paid was too high. We did what we thought was right. William chose to go out with me that day, knowing the dangers. Without his bravery, three good men would have perished. Do what you believe in, son, and hang the opinions of others."

The words often popped into Henry's head, long after his father was gone. "Do what you believe in, son, and hang the opinions of others."

The morning after he had survived his own storm - and been clipped around the ear by Penrose for his troubles - Henry packed a canvas bag and quietly left Mousehole forever. His mother, Anne, was away attending to her midwifery duties;

he thought twice about leaving a note and decided against it, often wishing afterwards that he had done so.

For protection and good fortune, he tucked into his boot his father's sheathed fishing knife, the special one with the ivory handle.

It took him a little over an hour on foot, via the rival fishing port of Newlyn, to reach Penzance. The bustling port town, Henry knew, offered him the best chance of securing sea passage to Portsmouth.

There were several large boats in the harbour, their bare masts rocking gently with the loping waves. Henry spotted one being loaded with crates and headed for it, contentedly whistling an old sea shanty. It feels good to be master of my own destiny at last, *he thought to himself.*

The vessel, the Mary Belle, was a 60-foot merchant ketch with two masts, sturdy enough to withstand the English Channel's squalls. Its hull was green with white trim, and its captain, Richard Hawke, was on deck, supervising the loading operation. When he noticed Henry standing there, he cocked his head towards him.

Henry took the hint. "I'm making for Portsmouth, sir. Are you heading that way?"

"Aye, then on to London," replied Hawke, weighing him up. "You look like a sturdy young lad. I could use an extra pair of hands on deck."

Henry grinned and threw his bag to the captain. "Much obliged to you, sir. I'll work hard for my passage!"

Hawke held out his hand; Henry took it and stepped down into the Mary Belle, taking extra care not to stumble.

"That you will, lad," replied the captain when they were face-to-face. "What business have you in Portsmouth?"

Henry removed his knitted wool cap and scrunched it in his hands. "I plan to join the King's navy, sir."

Chapter Thirteen

The Plague Museum

When they were safely outside the chandlery, the inquisitors shook their heads in disbelief. Jacob removed his hat and periwig and ran a hand through his sweaty, short, matted hair. Abby vigorously rubbed her eyes.

It was a while before either of them could speak.

Jacob exhaled. "She must be the Plague Doctor," he said.

Abby produced a large iron key from her satchel and held it up. "If that is so, then why would she so readily give up the key to her Plague Museum?"

"The woman has lost her wits!"

It was hard to disagree.

"We should make haste to her grim museum," Jacob said. "I fancy we shall find clues aplenty there."

The sky had clouded over while they were inside the chandlery, and drizzle began to fall. As they retraced their steps towards the dockyard, Abby asked, "Did you feel pity for her, Jacob?"

"Did you lose family to the plague?" he replied.

As well he knew, none of her three brothers had survived childhood, and her mother had died giving birth to the youngest. Sent on remand to the notorious Clink jail on trumped-up charges, her father had succumbed there to scurvy. Her only known relatives in Greenwich, with whom she had spent two contented years of clean air and learning, she had not seen since her employment by Mr Pepys.

But Jacob's question had been rhetorical. Before she could answer, he went on, "Rare is the citizen who did not witness the death of a dear one at the hand of that foul miasma. Though my father sent me out of London, that I might escape its grip…"

"Jacob, what is your point?"

"That all of London was touched by tragedy, and that some coped better than others. Only one, with whom we are familiar, resorted to murder. The plague doctor, Lydia Mercer."

Abby winced, unconvinced, just as a rat-faced man with a pigtail and gold earring passed her, slapping her thigh and smirking as he did so.

She glared at his receding form. He walked, she noticed, with a limp.

The inquisitors almost missed the museum, so small and unassuming was it, and overshadowed on either side by warehouses that were two tall storeys high. They assumed it had once been a night watchman's office, or the temporary base of a dockyard official. It had the air of a refuge, set on a single floor with a dilapidated thatched roof that housed nesting gulls.

So weathered and faded was the signage that it was only when the inquisitors drew close that they could make out the lettering:

Mercer's Plague Museum

The constant background hammering and clattering seemed strangely subdued there, perhaps muffled by the tall warehouses. The River Thames at their backs, teeming with sail-boats running with the tide, lapped against the wooden embankment, and the river birds officiously honked and quacked. It was all rather eerie.

"Where is everybody?" Abby asked.

It was hard to find anywhere not milling with menfolk around the docks. Yet here: not a soul.

While she was lost in the stillness of the moment, Jacob tried the door. Finding it locked, he loudly rattled the handle, barging it with his shoulder.

"Jacob! Lydia Mercer gave us the key!" she reminded him, hunting in her satchel.

"Forgive me," he said, shaking his head. "I fear that recent events have befuddled my mind."

Abby turned the key into the lock. "I confess I'm apprehensive," she told Jacob as the door creaked open.

There were four windows along each of the two longest walls. All bore shutters, a few of them so loose or broken that they admitted dim shafts of light, in which dust particles meandered. On the far wall, facing them, was another door. The whole place smelled damp.

The space was lined with tables and wooden display cases, and the walls were covered in framed and unframed notices and handbills. In the centre were more tables. The room was divided into four sections, each noted by a large printed sign: 'Medical Equipment'; 'Victims' Belongings'; 'Quarantine Practices'; and 'Charity Work'.

Neglect had taken its toll. Two of the tables had collapsed, distributing their exhibits across the floor. Rain had come in through the roof and ruined a display of notices, which lay half-disintegrated on the wooden floor.

The inquisitors stood in the doorway, surveying the sad scene. Abby could hear her heart beating. After a significant period of contemplation, they stepped as one into the room, Abby moving to the left and Jacob to the right.

He found himself in the Charity Work section. On the tables, he saw pamphlets advertising Mercer's Aid for the Afflicted and dozens of letters of gratitude from families the charity had helped. On the wall was a framed list of donors: Deptford merchants and shopkeepers, private benefactors, naval institutions, and, he was pleased to see, the name 'Samuel Pepys'.

Everything was covered in a layer of dust, which he felt he dare not disturb. *Have I misjudged Lydia Mercer?* he wondered.

Abby, meanwhile, was inspecting the items in the Victims' Belongings area. She was experiencing the same reluctance to touch as Jacob, as if everything on display in the museum were a precious holy relic, or perhaps nervous of reawakening the plague itself. A pervading sense of reverence inhabited the space. Were the owners of these otherwise ordinary trinkets and treasures watching her? She found herself looking up and around.

Cheap jewellery, tobacco tins and engraved keepsakes were displayed in a glass-fronted case, each with a handwritten label. On the tables, Abby saw hats, gloves, bags, a yellowing lace handkerchief initialled 'EH', a prayer book... Her eyes were drawn to one specific object: a small, hand-stitched rag doll with two button eyes, in a simple, threadbare dress. Compelled to do so, she picked it up and read the label:

This doll belonged to Mary Jarvis, aged 7, who succumbed to the plague along with her family. Found clutched in her arms when the house was opened after quarantine.

Those button eyes… They seemed to know. Gently, she replaced the doll, walked solemnly across to Jacob, and tapped him on the back. He started with a shriek.

"We should leave," she told him, her voice thick with emotion.

"Have you found a clue?" he asked.

Abby shook her head. "What do we even seek, Jacob?"

He surveyed the room.

"All her exhibits are labelled and attributed," Abby said quietly. "She didn't steal them."

Although less than fully convinced, Jacob felt unable to argue the point. "We must at least check that door at the far end," he said.

It turned out to be locked. Taking one step back, Jacob shoulder-barged the door. It flew open, scattering clouds of dust and cobwebs.

It was the first thing they both saw: the long waxed, hooded robe in black hanging from the wall opposite. A wooden cane was leaning against it, and on the floor were a wide-brimmed leather hat, gloves and a plague doctor's mask.

"She concealed it from us," said Jacob. "Behind a locked door. Why is it not displayed among the other things?"

"Yet she admits she wore it," Abby pointed out.

They were about to step into the room when Jacob thrust an arm out to halt his fellow inquisitor. "Hold!" he exclaimed, staring at the floor.

"What is it?"

Jacob pointed back along the route they had taken through the museum. "What do you notice?" he asked.

She shrugged. "A museum."

"Look at the floor."

"Footprints? In the dust?"

Jacob's and Abby's footprints were clearly visible in the thick layer of dust that covered the dark floorboards, indicating that they were the first visitors in quite some time.

"Aye! Now what do you see here?" he asked, pointing at the similarly timbered floorspace in the back-room.

The dust layer had all but disappeared. At the far end, illuminated only by the light through the door Jacob had barged open, was a crumpled blanket. Beside that was another door.

"Somebody slept here," Abby said.

Treading carefully so as not to disturb what little foot-print evidence remained, Abby made her way to the door and tried the handle. It opened. Jacob saw her walk out, return, and then touch her palm to an unlit leaded-glass lantern hanging beside the door.

"'Tis warm," she said. "Whoever was here, they left in a hurry."

The inquisitors were able to discern two part-foot-prints: one, that of a smaller man's or larger woman's shoe, nearer the internal door; and another, merely the impression of the toe area of a boot, noticeably much larger, definitely a man's, nearer the external door.

"What can it mean?" Jacob asked.

"It seems we have two people in this room," Abby replied.

Jacob's eyes widened. "Two Plague Doctors?"

"We must not leap to conclusions," she warned him. "This room and that plague-doctor garb may have no connection with the murders."

Jacob picked up the mask. While he had seen them worn on a few occasions, he had never held one nor been able to inspect one so closely.

The leather was thick and stiff, to cover the exposed face and keep out the foul air. The eye-holes were round glass set into a brass rim. That grotesque beak, a foot long and tapering.

Warily, as if it might attach itself to him and never let go, Jacob fitted the mask over his head. Instantly claustrophobic, he snatched it away, having caught just a faint hint of the dried herbs packed into the beak's tip.

Abby picked up the hat and gloves. She had no intention of trying them on.

Jacob noticed her intently scratching one of the glove's fingertips. "What have you found?"

She showed him. Dark, russet-red scrapings in the palm of her hand, almost black.

"Is it blood?" he asked, taking the glove from her. Sniffing them both, he pushed one under her nose.

"Gunpowder," she said quietly.

Chapter Fourteen

Peter Bradshaw

It was mid-afternoon when they returned to The Ship, their bellies empty and their heads filled with more questions than answers. Although they were late for the usual dinner time, the tables in the ground-floor tap-room were nearly all occupied – not that many were eating. Arthur Hall, behind his counter, smirked as they entered.

"Ignore the dullard," said Jacob.

Abby nudged him. "Hedges," she said, pointing at two men seated opposite one another.

The warehouse owner waved, and his companion turned around to see who he was greeting.

"That's the man we recently saw near the plague museum," Jacob told Abby. "The one who slapped you."

"Is that Bradshaw?" she asked herself, as she marched towards the two men.

Jacob quickly followed.

"Will you join us?" Hedges asked the inquisitors, motioning towards two spare chairs.

While Jacob hesitated, Abby needed no further bidding. "You must be Alfred Bradshaw," she said, praying that she was right.

"Aye," the pigtailed man replied, eyeing her intently. "And you must be the Harcourt girl and Standish, of whom we've heard so many tales. Samuel Pepys's esteemed inquisitors don't look up to much to me."

An awkward silence descended.

Bradshaw wore a gold earring in his left ear and a cutlass in his belt. He had shifty grey eyes, a scarred face and a pock-marked nose. His tousled ginger hair was plaited into a pigtail that fell down his back, and he had a wispy ginger beard. Peter Bradshaw was a man you would not wish to meet in a dark alleyway.

"You're a merchant?" Abby asked him, having pictured someone considerably more upstanding. "What do you trade in?"

He leered at her. "What do you require?"

Quick as a flash, she replied, "Plague-doctor garb and a pistol."

Bradshaw and Hedges roared with laughter, slapping the table in delight. "Arthur!" Hedges called to the innkeeper. "Fetch these landlubbers a drink!"

Abby did not dare refuse the offer, though she had no intention of repeating the previous night's revelry.

"Who will pay, you or I?" Hedges asked his companion, producing a pair of dice from his pocket. Rolling them across the table, he eagerly inspected the result. "Two and a four," he announced, somewhat deflated.

Bradshaw cackled, retrieved the dice, and blew on them in his cupped hands. "I'll not be buying these wastrels their ale!" He rolled. "Six and five! Your shout, loser!"

Buoyed by his partner's brazen line in questioning, Jacob chanced his own hand. "We were told that bad blood exists betwixt yourselves, Drake and Wilkes."

He noticed a look pass between the two men.

"Nay. No bad blood 'twixt us and Wilkes," Bradshaw growled back. "On account of him being dead."

Jacob sneered. "Dead by whose hand?"

Bradshaw glared at him. "Not by my hand, if that is what you insinuate!"

"What about Drake?" asked Abby.

Bradshaw laughed in her face. "Drake? Wouldn't frighten a babe in arms! He's little bigger than a boy!"

"Calm yourself, Peter," said Hedges.

Bradshaw ignored him and stood menacingly.

Jacob rose in response, looming inevitably taller. Not that his opponent appeared troubled by the height difference. "Do you accuse me of murder?" Bradshaw demanded, fingering his cutlass handle.

Abby motioned for both men to be seated; neither obeyed. "We accuse no one, Mr Bradshaw," she assured him. "My fellow inquisitor has had a troubling day and speaks out of turn."

Arthur Hall appeared at their table with two tankards. "I see you're befriending the locals," he quipped, grinning at Jacob.

"Come, Arthur, we should return to our work," said Hedges. "A pleasure to make your acquaintance once again, Abigail Harcourt."

She held up a finger. "Before you depart, sir, one further question?"

Hedges nodded.

"Are you aware of gambling here at The Ship? We were told that Wilkes had debts."

Hedges and Wilkes eyed the dice on the table. Hedges scooped them up and returned them to his pocket. "Don't you know that gambling's regulated?" he replied.

"Why don't you ask Arthur there?" added Bradshaw, winking. As he left, he suddenly feigned a lunge at Jacob, who managed not to flinch. With a satisfied nod, he was gone.

Hedges followed, leaning first to whisper into Abby's ear, "Ask the foreign singer what she did in Tangier."

"I do not trust Bradshaw," Jacob told Abby, greedily tucking into a plate of mutton with mashed turnip. "Did you notice he walks with a limp, like the Plague Doctor whom Maggie Wilkes witnessed? He also passed us outside the Plague Museum. Might it have been he who left by the back door, ere we entered?"

She was already halfway through a meat pie. "I certainly don't trust him, but there are holes in your theory, Jacob. The Plague Doctor we saw did not limp…"

"I did not see him," Jacob replied, "since I was…" He trailed off.

"But I *did* see him, and I swear he was not limping."

"Can you be certain?"

"'Tis possible I'm mistaken," she conceded. "But as you yourself said, injuries may heal. Wilkes was murdered a while ago, and the Plague Doctor's limp may not be permanent."

"Then what of Lydia Mercer? There was dried blood and an odour of gunpowder on her plague doctor's gloves," he pointed out.

"The blood was old, Jacob. It might have been there for months, since the plague itself."

"And the gunpowder?"

"More troubling," she conceded. "However, somebody, we can be sure, was living in that back-room of the Plague Museum. It could be anybody in that plague-doctor garb, not only Lydia."

"Then what of her paintings, of her husband and sons? They were most disturbing. Lydia Mercer saw too much during that wretched time and became touched in the head. Though she is a woman, I strongly believe murder is within her means."

With a sigh, Abby retrieved her notebook from her satchel. "As it stands, we have several suspects to consider," she said, and she wrote them down.

Hugo Hedges and Peter Bradshaw

Known to have fallen out with Wilkes and Drake over accusations of treason aboard a royal naval vessel returning from Tangier.

Lydia Mercer

Suspected by Theodore Penn and Nora Drake. Penn mentioned Mercer dressing as a plague doctor when she was denounced as a dangerous charlatan. Nora Drake recalled the chandler's feud with Wilkes and her husband over accusations of theft and profiteering. The two men confined Mercer's family in their home during the plague, leading to their deaths.

Arthur Hall

Accused by Kitty Blake, claiming Wilkes and Drake had once fought with the innkeeper over land requisitioned from him as a plague pit, leaving Hall with serious injuries.

Kitty Blake

Named by Penn and later Hedges. Both hinted at sinister dealings in Tangier. A direct link with Wilkes and Drake remains elusive. Too slight in stature to convincingly play the Plague Doctor, she would need to hire an assassin to act the part. Could such a demure woman be capable of such a scheme?

Chapter Fifteen

Secrets & Lies

"Did I hear my name spoken?"

The inquisitors immediately recognised the mellifluous tone.

Kitty Blake smiled as she took the seat next to Jacob, recently vacated by Hugo Hedges. Hastily, Abby stuffed her book of notes back into her satchel.

Jacob coughed and found sudden interest in a lump of gristle extracted from one of his sausages.

Abby belatedly returned Kitty's smile. "There are men in Deptford who would see you jailed," she told her.

"My dear, there are men in Deptford who would see me dead," Kitty replied, sounding entirely unperturbed. "They do not take kindly to the colour of my skin."

"Might it be more than that?" Abby persisted.

Kitty pulled a tasselled, multicoloured silk scarf from her shoulders, adjusted her long hair, and wrapped it around her head. "Have you visited Tangier?" she asked, already knowing the answer. "It is a most beautiful city on the shore of the Gibraltar Strait, bathed in golden sunlight. It is the gateway between Africa and Europe and bustles with ships. All life is there: Berber, Arab, Moor, English, Spanish, French... There are tensions!" she laughed.

Jacob was so lost in the sound of her voice that he leaned backwards on his stool, expecting to encounter a wall behind him, but misjudged the distance and toppled over. There he sat sheepishly, hoping the singer might find him endearing.

Instead she ignored him completely and continued, "When I was a child, I would play in the narrow, cobbled streets around the great fortress we call the Kasbah. It is the heart of Tangier, built on top of a high hill overlooking the sea. An enchanting place I hold dear to my heart."

Jacob, who had retaken his stool, asked, "Why did you leave?"

"Ha!" she exclaimed. "That is another story."

It was a story the inquisitors needed to hear. But how to coax it from her?

"Who wishes you dead, Kitty?" Abby asked. "Hugo Hedges? Peter Bradshaw?"

But the singer was wise to her, expressionless.

Abby would have to try harder, she realised. "We can help," she said.

A barely perceptible tilt of Kitty's head suggested Abby might have found a chink in her armour.

"How can you help?" Kitty asked, sounding unconvinced.

Jacob saw his chance to impress. "Miss Blake," he said, brushing at his coat sleeve. "We are the personal inquisitors of Mr Samuel Pepys."

She regarded him blankly.

"*Mr Samuel Pepys?*" he repeated more loudly.

The singer threw her arms in the air. "Raising your voice will not make me familiar with this man!"

Jacob was obliged to explain Pepys's position as Clerk of the Acts and his connection to Deptford. "He is one of the most powerful men in the King's navy," he assured her. "And a close acquaintance of mine," he added (having only met Pepys a fortnight ago).

At least it got her attention. "He could find me a new position, away from this stinking inn and its vulgar customers?" Kitty asked.

Jacob was taken aback. He rather liked the place, the innkeeper aside. *It has colour!* he thought. *What more does this foreigner expect?* He was about to voice as much when Abby butted in.

"Aye," she said, taking Kitty's hand. "I'm sure he can help you." She looked towards Jacob, hoping he would back her up.

Frankly, he found it highly unlikely that the Clerk of the Acts to the Navy Board would help secure a singer from Tangier the post of her desires. Fortunately, however, he registered Abby's prompting. "Aye," he confirmed, shifting his periwig slightly. "What position did you have in mind?"

She gazed into his eyes, causing him to sigh involuntarily. "Translator," she replied. "I speak eight languages: Arabic, Tamazight, Darija, English, French, Spanish, Portuguese and Dutch."

"Odd's fish!" Jacob heard himself exclaim.

"*Je voudrais visiter les beaux pays de la monde.*"

To his astonishment, it was Abby who had spoken the words, which were entirely meaningless to him.

Kitty smiled, yet her eyes were puzzled. "*Vouz parlez Francaise!*"

The young inquisitor blushed. "*Seulement un peu,*" she admitted. "*La famille de la femme de* Master Pepys, Elizabeth…," she struggled for the right words. "*Ils sont de la France?*"

"*Ils sont* de *France,*" Kitty corrected her. "Your master's wife's family are from France? And she teaches you?"

"Nay!" Abby exclaimed a little too loudly. "Nay. I learn with Master Pepys."

"*Your master teaches you?*" Kitty asked, amazed.

"He's a kind gentleman," she replied quietly. "*Et maintenant. S'il vous plait, dite-nous ce qui s'est passé en Tangier.*"

"*C'est à Tanger, pas en Tangier,*" the singer corrected her again.

"Merci." Abby turned to Jacob, who was beside himself with admiration. "I asked her to tell us what happened in Tangier."

Warily, Kitty began her tale...

After Tangier was acquired by Charles II in 1661, the King's ships began to arrive, flying their British ensigns. For Kitty, working as go-between for her family of merchants, it opened up new opportunities and fresh trade routes.

The English, she discovered, had a taste for Moroccan silks, leather and ceramics, and for exotic spices such as saffron and cumin, as well as sugar and tobacco. She arranged imports into Tangier of machinery and textiles - wool, cotton, linen - and for her wealthier customers, English silverware. Business was good.

Besides the great merchant ships, Royal Navy galleons sailed to and from the port, bringing in supplies of men as they built up the British garrison and city defences.

Singing in Tangier's bars at night, as was her pleasure, she came to know several of these navy seamen on a personal level. It was how Kitty ended up meeting the English sea captain who became her lover.

Abby interrupted her tale. "What was his name?"

"His name was Henry," she replied. "Meeting him changed everything for me in Tangier."

Her parents had arranged a marriage for her, Kitty said, with the son of a wealthy rival Moroccan merchant. Their plan was to unite the two businesses and create the largest trading company in Tangier. She was 30 years old, fiercely independent, and unmotivated by wealth. Her suitor, she found a bore.

"He would talk only of money and trade and the many children we would have together. I wanted adventure," she said.

One day in late 1664, when Henry's ship, the Venturer, was due to set sail, she asked the captain if she could travel with him to England. It would be risky for them both, she knew. He would have to stow her away on board, keeping her presence a secret from all but one or two trusted crew members. The risks for Kitty were also high, since she would be trapped in a sweltering, custom-built hideaway in the hold, among the bilge water, supplies and rats.

If found out, the captain faced a court martial and Kitty, possibly worse. "They might have thrown me overboard," she pointed out matter-of-factly.

The journey to Deptford took five gruelling weeks, but she was a fighter, and she survived. "The bosun brought me bread and water once a day, that was all," Kitty explained. "Every time he visited, we knew I might be seen."

It was only once they were on dry land that Henry told her of the skullduggery that had taken place during the trip. "A sailor had spied me in the hold," Kitty recalled. "I don't know how or when; I did not see him. He recognised me from Tangier and knew who would be responsible for smuggling me aboard. Afterwards, he blackmailed Henry."

"Who was this sailor?" Abby asked.

Kitty held a finger to her lips. "No more names, Abigail. I have talked too much. Talk is dangerous in Deptford - it costs lives. Bring your Mr Pepys to me. When he makes me his translator, then I will tell you the rest of my story."

"We were told something happened in Tangier," Abby pressed her. "Something bad."

"You were told wrong, my dear." Kitty got up from her stool. "Now, I must sing for my supper."

With that, Kitty Blake - Katharina Al-Yazid - drifted elegantly to the far corner of the tap-room, where she began her preparations to entertain the rabble.

"Somebody's lying to us," said Abby.

Shifting to the seat opposite her, Jacob beckoned Abby in close. "I noticed something as Kitty donned her headscarf," he said, looking around to ensure no one was eavesdropping. "She has a strange blue symbol inked behind her left ear."

"What symbol?"

"It appeared to be a crescent moon."

When she opened her mouth to congratulate him, he stopped her. "There is more." He paused, milking the moment. "Bradshaw has his hair plaited, which allowed me to see that he also has a symbol inked behind the same ear. It appeared to be a rabbit."

Chapter Sixteen

Kentish Knock

*S*eventeen-year-old Henry Trevelyan set out from Portsmouth in 1641, fired up to fight for king and country. It was his duty, he considered, as a proud Englishman.

Fate and the future had different plans for him.

Henry began his training as a gunner's mate aboard the Lionheart. He quickly discovered that taking charge of a small fishing boat bore no resemblance to manning a muzzle-loading cannon on a royal warship.

The first few weeks opened his eyes. He slept in a hammock in cramped, squalid conditions below deck; ate food that was tasteless or rotting; was paid a pittance; swabbed the decks; learned how to furl and unfurl sails and to work the rigging; mastered firing a musket and handling a cutlass; and spent hour upon hour training to clean, load and fire the heavy bronze cannon. Night-watch duty meant he rested only fitfully. He had not even fired a shot in anger.

Yet he embraced the life. It gave him a true purpose and a cause to stand behind. When his thoughts drifted back to

Cornwall, those early years felt diminished to him - a pointless, grinding subsistence. If only my father could see me now, *he thought.* And Peck. And that sanctimonious harbour-master, Robert Penrose. *He longed to sail past Mousehole and call out from high in the rigging, "Look at me now!"*

The following year, King Charles's battle for control with Parliament reached a stalemate that resulted in Civil War, pitting royalist against parliamentarian, Englishman against Englishman. Trevelyan's visions of leaping to the defence of his monarch were swiftly shattered when the majority of the navy sided with the King's opponents.

It was a new cause that he would grow to embrace. The King sought autonomy at the expense of his citizens' rights; more-over, he had married a Roman Catholic, the Frenchwoman, Henrietta Maria, and many feared a return to the old religion.

The Lionheart helped to patrol the English coastline, pro-tecting its trade routes and supplying parliamentarian gar-risons. To Henry's dismay, the bulk of the fighting took place inland.

Only when he was transferred to the Mary Rose did he finally experience battle, and he was itching for it.

In late April 1644, his warship was sent to aid the par-liamentarian commander, Robert Blake's forces, defending the garrison at Lyme Regis in Dorset.

The Mary Rose weighed anchor, and Henry found himself rowing ashore to take up a musket against the royalist attackers led by Prince Rupert. Fighting among his crew-mates, not much older than himself, he discovered an innate talent for leadership.

As the outer defences of the town were breached, Henry took charge of his small band of sailors, fortifying a strategic building and repelling a fierce royalist assault. When the smoke had cleared, just one of his group had been killed, while the enemy forces lay dead and dying around them. Henry surprised even himself.

His quick wits and bravery were noted. Robert Blake sought him out afterwards to commend his decisive action and to offer support for the young man's naval career. Henry's subsequent rise through the ranks was meteoric, overseen by his influential mentor.

He discovered that he relished danger and thrived on hardship. The greater the chaos, the calmer his demeanour. He led from the front and inspired his men. Having worked his way up the chain of command rather than infiltrating it through family ties, he understood the desires and quibbles of the ordinary seaman and judged their actions accordingly.

The name Henry Trevelyan became feted among the naval community, and men actively sought to sail on his ships.

His most celebrated action, which was recounted for years after, occurred at the Battle of Kentish Knock during the Dutch War in 1652. Henry was by then serving as a lieutenant aboard the 64-gun Vanguard, as part of Oliver Cromwell's

Commonwealth forces under the command of his old mentor, Blake.

The Dutch and English ships met in the North Sea, some 20 miles east of the mouth of the River Thames. Although the Dutch were marginally outnumbered, the bulky English ships found manoeuvring practically impossible in the light winds. As the cannons engaged, two of the navy's finest vessels, including the 90-gun Sovereign, ran aground on a sandbank.

As the Dutch warships closed in and the prospect of victory slipped away, Henry volunteered to sail a burning fireship into the enemy's midst. Sacrificing one English ship for the chance of destroying multiple enemy vessels, it was, however, a suicide mission. Despite that, crewmen lined up to accompany Henry, and he picked the two-dozen most dependable.

An old merchant vessel had been loaded with vast quantities of oil, gunpowder and rags, to be ignited at just the right moment. Too early, and the fireship's own sails would be destroyed, halting its progress; too late, and the quarry might escape before the flames from the burning fireship could travel to their vessels.

Stealth and disguise were key. Dummy wooden cannons protruded from the merchantman's gun-ports, to make it appear like any other warship. Two 'sally-ports' had been cut into either side of the ship, near the stern, to allow the crew to escape into rowing boats towed behind them.

The Vanguard's captain tried forbidding Henry to attempt the mission, telling him, "Your men are better served by you *as Lieutenant of this ship, not embarking upon a foolhardy venture that can lead only to your certain death."*

But he would not be dissuaded, his father's words ringing in his ears: "Do what you believe in, son, and hang the opinions of others."

Boarding the fireship with his men, Henry dispatched his loyal crew to their various stations. Some to the tiller, others to the rigging and a handful to the working cannons. He would man the quarter deck, guiding the vessel with hollered commands, and light the fuse that would turn their ship into a massive, floating fireball.

Henry could see a cluster of Dutch warships advancing on the stricken *Sovereign*, their sails flapping limply in the breeze. Explosions were going off all around him, and a pall of ash-grey smoke hung heavily over the scene.

Using all his years of experience at sea, going back to the earliest trips out with his father aboard *Anne's Hope*, Henry studied the cloud formations and the waves.

"Tiller to starboard!" he yelled to the men below, forecasting what he dearly hoped would be a change in the wind direction. The cheers from his crew rang out as their fireship lurched forward, its sails billowing magnificently, the British flag fluttering proudly on its bowsprit.

A pair of frigates were escorting the fireship, and they let loose their cannon fire. The Dutch, still drifting haphazardly, returned fire. The hull of Henry's fireship was hit several times, *punching holes in its side, sending deadly splinters flying in all directions.*

As they closed in on their quarry the escorting frigates, with the wind now at their backs, peeled off, and the fireship was left on its own. When Henry could make out the faces of the enemy's crews, he abandoned his post and raced down steep, narrow sets of wooden steps towards the gunpowder barrels piled on the orlop deck. As he did so, he called to his men, "To the sally-ports!"

Reaching the fuse, he stood there with his flint and steel in that dark and musty space. It occurred to him that this must have been Guy Fawkes's experience as he prepared to blow up Parliament. Almost 50 years later, here he was, fighting as a parliamentarian.

While explosions continued to ring out and the fireship rocked with every direct hit at close range, time stood still for Henry. He sensed only utter silence.

His first spark failed to catch on the oil-soaked rags. And the second. "Ignite, you fool! Ignite!" he cursed. The third spark caught with a satisfying 'whoomph'.

Henry Trevelyan ran for his life, as he had never run before. His eyes were alive to every obstacle. One false step, a single trip, and he might be done for.

Approaching a sally-port, he heard the calls of his crewmen, who were already waiting for him in their small escape craft.

"Sir!"

"Mr Trevelyan, hurry!"

Forceful yet not panicked, just as he had trained them.

The Dutch were routed at the Battle of Kentish Knock, and Henry's daredevil action was cited as the decisive factor. The Sovereign was saved and the English were victorious. Cromwell himself demanded to meet the navy's new hero, and presented him with a bag of gold coins.

Robert Blake promoted Henry to the rank of captain and gave him his own 80-gun ship to command: the Venturer.

The Cornishman had reached the peak of his powers.

Chapter Seventeen

Night Flight

The inquisitors retired early to their guest chambers at The Ship, well before the local church bell tolled nine. Both were acclimatising to the intensity and stress of their new roles. At least Jacob had been promised a decent wage (not that Mr Pepys had yet handed over any money). Abigail was still on her housemaid's pay of a shilling a week! When possible, she would approach her master about the matter.

Up two flights of battered wooden stairs, the top floor of the inn bore a distinct odour. Was it sweaty feet? Mouldy stockings? Unlaundered linen? Rotten fish? Or a combination of them all?

Although the constant barrage of shipbuilding sounds ceased after dark, Deptford did not fall silent by any means. Seafarers enjoyed cavorting, and the two floors between Jacob and the main tap-room did nothing to lessen the volume of the revellers below. He fancied he could hear Kitty's singing and the roared approval, as if she were in the chamber beside him. *If only*, he thought.

He shuttered his window, set down his bag and sat heavily on the bed... if the wooden frame packed with old sailcloth could be classified as such. The single candle Arthur Hall had begrudgingly handed him illuminated the room in flickers. The innkeeper was frugal with the decorative touches. No looking glass, no desk, no stool, no wall hangings. Just a chamber pot in the corner of the room.

Jacob removed his scuffed brown leather shoes, promising himself that he would replace them with a more fashionable pair - the latest small, oval buckles had caught his eye - just as soon as he was paid. Next, he removed his coat and laid it on the grimy wooden floor, reasoning that it could hardly become any dirtier. On top of that, he placed his hat and trusty periwig.

His waistcoat, shirt and breeches, he kept on. The nights had grown cold and there was no fireplace in the room.

Mulling over their first full day in Deptford, he felt contented by what they had achieved. As Abby had promised him after their first, faltering investigation into Mr Pepys's stolen diaries, he was indeed growing in confidence and composure. He had much to thank her for but decided he would not do so, in case it seemed too forward. Their relationship was strictly business, he assured himself.

There had been romantic liaisons in his past, although none had lasted. *I always seem to be the one discarded*, he thought to himself, *not the one doing the discarding*. Raising his hand to adjust his periwig, he remembered that he had taken it off.

Jacob sighed to himself and laid down. His feet hung out over the end of the bed-frame, which cut uncomfortably into his ankles. Pulling the single grey woollen blanket over himself, he blew out his candle and instantly fell fast asleep.

Jacob woke with a start; the room was pitch black and all was quiet. Disoriented, he pushed himself up.

What hour is this? he wondered.

No glimmer of daylight came through the gaps in the weather-beaten window shutters. It felt like the early hours of the morning.

So why have I woken?

Feeling blindly with his right hand, he sought his candle, nudged it, and heard it roll across the floor away from him.

"Gah!" he muttered to himself.

Twisting around, he set his feet down and realised he had trodden on his hat.

Suddenly he sensed something... Sitting stock still, he listened intently, straining his ears. Was there somebody in the room with him? Was that a faint, muffled breathing he had caught?

"Is somebody there?" he asked quietly.

No reply came.

His every sense now alert, he felt a tingle at the nape of his neck. Swallowing dryly, he peered into the void, willing his eyes to see.

"Is somebody there?" he asked again.

Nothing.

Jacob rose to his feet and began walking towards the far wall, hands stretched out before him, negotiating the darkness. When he judged that he had travelled the length of the chamber, his hand encountered something solid... *Yet it is neither wooden nor flat, like a wall should be,* he thought. *This is...* He moved his other hand so that both could work to identify the incongruous obstacle.

The material at my fingertips... Is it leather? It appears to be conical-shaped... It grew wider as his hands moved forward, sensing curved sheets of leather, covering something solid. *And there...?* He tapped the cold, hard surface his fingers had encountered. *It sounds like... like glass.*

The dawning realisation engulfed him like an icy wave.

I am holding the Plague Doctor's head.

Before he could react, he felt himself being pushed violently backwards and toppled, reeling, to the floor. The back of his head smacked into the hard wood, sending his mind spinning. He heard his door wrenched open and footsteps diminishing.

A thin, warm light from lanterns on the corridor wall outside entered his room, and finally Jacob was able to see. Without a second thought, he was up and away, on the trail of the fleeing Plague Doctor.

Launching himself down the stairs, he emerged into the dimly lit tap-room just as the dark, robed figure of the Plague Doctor bolted through the main door, slamming it behind him. The nearby church bell chimed twice.

His attention focused on the doorway, he failed to notice the upended stool in the middle of the floor, left there by his quarry. His foot caught on one of the wooden legs, sending him crashing into the nearest table, cheek-first, and he cried out in pain.

Ignoring the pain, he swung open the door; in his peripheral vision he noticed a piece of paper on the floor, beside the door frame. *Did the Plague Doctor drop that in his haste?* he wondered. Apprehending the fiend being paramount, he decided to retrieve it later and continued the chase.

Outside in the dockyard, a near-full moon cast a bright, silver light, creating ominous shadows from the most innocuous of objects. A chill enveloped the inquisitor, which he shrugged off.

The otherworldly silence was broken only by the fleeing steps of the Plague Doctor. Jacob heard his prey but could not see him. The footsteps echoed, their rhythm unsteady, as if his prey were having trouble running.

Glancing about frantically, he spotted the murderer heading for the Great Storehouse, which loomed large and foreboding in the silvery light, some 100 yards ahead. "Hold, scoundrel!" he called out.

The Plague Doctor stopped, turned, and levelled a pistol at Jacob, who ducked just as the shot rang out. By the time the inquisitor had recovered his composure, his quarry had vanished.

Setting off at a sprint, Jacob trod on a sharp stone, yelped, hopping, and clutched his foot. It dawned on him: his feet were bare.

There was no time to return to his room and retrieve his shoes, so he continued the pursuit more gingerly, carefully checking the ground before him. His hopes of unmasking the Plague Doctor, he realised, were rapidly diminishing.

When he reached the Great Storehouse, Jacob slowed to a walk. The perimeter was timber-boarded, so his bare feet were safe now, even a boon, since he could tread without a sound. Having not seen the Plague Doctor enter any of the doors directly before him, Jacob walked around the corner of the huge building.

Two rows of windows lined the wall of the storehouse, which towered above Jacob. He tried the first door he came to, and, to his surprise, it opened. *Did the Plague Doctor do the same mere moments earlier?* he wondered.

Inside, lit by wall lanterns, was one great, high-ceilinged room, packed with piled naval supplies and equipment of every shape, size and description. Jacob stopped and listened out for movement, but heard only the scurrying of rats and mice.

With no choice but to hunt, he removed a lantern from a wall and set off between rows of stacked barrels and crates, which reached almost as high as the rafters. He passed piles of timber and coiled chains, bundles of hemp rope and stacks of canvas. Along the wall, shelving held an array of navigational instruments: compasses, quadrants, hourglasses, astrolabes.

He found crates of sailors' 'slops' - navy-issue clothing, caps, stockings, shirts, waistcoats, drawers - and, with sinking spirits, raked through a tall crate of shoes on the slender off-chance that his quarry might have secreted himself within. All Jacob discovered of note was an out-sized pair of boots that seemed to have no place among the navy-issue footwear.

The Plague Doctor could be anywhere, he thought to himself, *so vast is the number of hiding places.*

Suddenly, he heard a noise. Footsteps were heading his way, echoing amid the voluminous space. *Is that the Plague Doctor, believing he has eluded capture, brazenly heading home?* Jacob wondered.

His gaze fell on a row of cannon up ahead. Treading lightly for a man of his size, he reached it and concealed himself behind one of the largest guns. There, he waited, as the footsteps rounded a corner and drew nearer.

Peering out from behind a thick wooden carriage, he could make out the light from an approaching lantern dancing on the wall ahead of him. Jacob held his breath. He could feel his heart pumping in his chest, and his temples throbbed.

When the lantern light drew level with him, Jacob leapt from his hiding place. As he pounced, he became aware that the man he was about to reduce to a crumpled heap was not wearing plague-doctor garb. Instead, he was squat and grizzled, wearing a heavy woollen coat and carrying a cutlass.

It took several minutes before the night watchman would believe Jacob's story, having first subdued him and held him at cutlass-point. Fortunately, word of the Plague Doctor's notorious activities had done the rounds at the dockyard, adding credence to the inquisitor's jabbered words.

"A short while before I apprehended you, I heard footsteps on the other side of the storehouse from my office," the night watchman told Jacob. "When I called out, they fell silent. When I investigated, I saw a figure clad in black…"

"The Plague Doctor!" Jacob exclaimed.

"Nay!" replied the watchman, his mouth agog. "It never crossed my mind. *The Plague Doctor was here?*"

"Aye, sir. Which way did he go?

"I saw only the back of him, disappearing through that door." He pointed, walked to the door and opened it, peering out. "I gave chase, but he was too quick."

"Where was he heading?"

"Out towards the fields yonder. I couldn't desert my post, so I returned here and checked for signs of an accomplice. Not long afterwards, I heard you raking through supplies. 'Tis a busy night! Wait till I tell my wife I saw the Plague Doctor!"

With a heavy heart, Jacob returned to The Ship. His chance to unmask the criminal and solve the case single-handed had slipped through his fingers.

When he opened the inn door, he jumped. Arthur Hall was sitting there, waiting for him. Wearing just a nightshirt, the innkeeper looked sweaty and dishevelled.

"You startled me," Jacob told him, stepping inside.

"Good," Hall replied, smirking. He held out a piece of paper. "Lose something?"

Jacob checked: the paper he had spotted earlier was gone, so that must be it.

When he went to take it, the innkeeper snatched it away. "What's it mean?" he asked.

"I have no idea," Jacob replied, "having not yet seen it."

"Hmm," grunted Hall, handing it over.

It was a handwritten note, folded twice, that read:

H

Our friend of the watcher resides in Neptune's chariot. Request visit from the crow at midwatch.

The inquisitor felt sure that he recognised the hand.

Chapter Eighteen

Deep Down

As Arthur Hall disappeared through the back door, Jacob made his way upstairs to his chamber. When Hall's door closed, he stopped. Kitty Blake had told them he kept a weapon in an oak box on a shelf behind the counter; Abby had wondered aloud whether it might be a flintlock pistol, the Plague Doctor's weapon of choice.

Here is my chance to find out, he thought to himself.

The inn was unnaturally quiet.

On bare feet, Jacob tiptoed, as quietly as possible for a man of his size, to the innkeeper's habitual station. The shelf, positioned at the inquisitor's shoulder height, was lined with goblets and tankards, four vessels deep, yet no sign of an oak box. Had Kitty lied?

Then, idly lifting one of the tankards at the front, he saw it: the box. A row of tankards had concealed it from view. Jacob took the long, worn box down and laid it gently on the counter.

Inside, he found a flintlock pistol.

Picking it up, he sniffed the firing mechanism. The faintest whiff of gunpowder suggested that it had once been fired, although not recently. He would report back to Abby the moment she awoke.

As he replaced the box and concealed it behind tankards, just as he had found it, his ears caught the muffled sound of snoring. Unmistakably, it was the landlord, fallen into a deep slumber.

This, he decided, was a chance too good to miss.

Opening the back door very gingerly, Jacob found himself in a kitchen with a large fireplace. It smelled of hops, mildew and old meals and was filled with barrels, crates, pots and pans, lit dimly by an oil lamp on one wall. There was a door opposite, in the direction of the snoring, and another to his right.

Keen not to wake the innkeeper, he chose the latter.

Taking the lamp with him, he found himself descending a steep set of wooden stairs. The further he went, the colder and damper it felt. The sounds of his nervous breathing and Arthur's diminishing snores pounded in his ears. Jacob felt his hand shake and stopped to compose himself.

At the foot of the stairs, deeper beneath ground-floor level than he expected to go, the inquisitor came upon another door. Listening intently for sounds emanating from inside, he heard nothing. *Surely merely an abandoned cellar*, he thought to himself.

He was wrong, as it turned out. Very wrong.

When the thick oak door creaked open, Jacob was confronted by a room laid out with tables and stools, with a counter at the far end on which small, tapped barrels sat. The space smelled of stale ale, damp and lingering body odour. Water dripped from the wooden ceiling.

On one wall, in large white letters, was painted a slogan:

ROLL THE DICE
KILL OR DIE

Jacob's mouth fell open. He had discovered a hidden gambling den deep beneath The Ship.

Stepping slowly into the room, the inquisitor raised his lamp to better illuminate the space. The tables were rickety and stained, with rotting legs, strewn with dice and cards. There were knife cuts in some of the surfaces and Jacob wondered what drunken violence had occurred there, between seafarers fleeced of their wages on the roll of the dice.

When he went behind the counter, he found a shelf set into it. Among tankards and packs of cards, he found a small book, its pages thick and warped. Opening it, he found what looked to be a list of gambling debts on the last page:

Rat owes Quartermaster £2 6s 3d
Duck owes Raven £12 4s 2d
Hog owes Sow £5 8s 6d

"'Tis coded, Mr Standish. You will not understand its contents. Please replace it where you found it."

Startled, Jacob dropped the book.

Arthur Hall stood wreathed in shadows in the doorway, his flintlock pistol levelled at the inquisitor. "Would you take a stool?" he said.

As if Jacob had any choice.

The inquisitor's mind was racing as he waited for Arthur to pour them each an ale, then set two tankards down on his table and take a seat opposite.

If he ran, he knew that he would never make it up the steep steps without being shot at.

Could I tackle him? he wondered. The innkeeper was built like a fortress and armed to boot. It seemed unwise to try.

What if…?

"Let's play a game," said Arthur. His cold, brown eyes bore into Jacob's. He was wearing a thick wool coat over his nightshirt; his pistol, trained on Jacob's heart, looked tiny in his huge fist.

There were two dice on the table, which the innkeeper picked up with his free hand. "You see the code we live by, Mr Standish?" he asked, pointing at the words on the wall.

Jacob scanned it again.

ROLL THE DICE
KILL OR DIE

"I am the personal inquisitor of the Clerk of the Acts to the Navy, Mr Hall," Jacob said. "It would be unwise to trifle with me." He could hear his voice faltering.

Arthur smirked. "I know who you are, Jacob Standish. You are a failed purser with delusions of grandeur. Now, listen. These are the rules. You roll the dice then I roll the dice. If your total is higher, you live. If it is lower, then…" He clicked his tongue and shook his head.

"Sir, this is…" Jacob began to protest.

Hall slammed the dice down in front of him. "Roll." He pointed the gun between Jacob's eyes. "Or you die anyway."

The inquisitor looked at the dice: two smooth wooden cubes with pips burned into each surface to indicate the numbers. As they sat - showing four and six - even with his head for figures, he knew he had a strong chance of winning. Of saving his own life.

"May I keep these numbers?" he asked.

Arthur's chuckle was a deep, rumbling thing that sounded as if it originated in a cave. "Roll the dice, Standish. Last chance."

The inquisitor's hand trembled as he picked up the wooden cubes. Closing his eyes, he threw. When both dice rolled off the other side of the table, Hall slammed his fist down. "Don't play games with me, you fool," he said, waving his pistol.

Jacob opted not to point out that he was naturally clumsy.

Holding his breath, he rolled again. On seeing a five on one dice, his eyes lit up… and closed when he saw the one of the other dice. Six. Of a possible 12. Arthur's tight lips curled into a smile.

The innkeeper retrieved the dice and rolled. In Jacob's tumbling mind, they travelled across the table in slow motion. His heart threatened to burst through his rib-cage, and his stomach ached.

When the dice stopped, he had to look twice. A two and a three. *A two and a three!*

Even with his lax head for figures, he knew he had won.

Wordlessly, Arthur rose and disappeared through the door.

Jacob slumped forward and cradled his head in his forearms.

Chapter Nineteen

The Morning After

J acob decided not to wake Abby, even though he ached to do so. Her sharp mind would be better used by them if fully rested, he knew. Yet he could not sleep, the events of the night churning through his thoughts, and he found himself tapping impatiently on her door the moment the church bell chimed its first of five.

"Jacob?" Abby enquired croakily, dampening her cracked lips with her tongue.

The next thing she knew, her shutters were flung open and Jacob plonked himself onto the end of her bed, landing squarely on her foot.

"Ow!" she exclaimed. "What do you want?"

"I have so much to tell," he said breathlessly, "I confess I know not where to begin."

Before she could protest, he dragged her out of bed and into the gloomy corridor.

"Look," he told her, pointing at his door.

Rubbing sleep from her eyes, Abby gasped.

Daubed upon Jacob's door in black paint was a large cross and the words, 'LORD HAVE MERCY UPON HIM'.

The tap-room was already busy with dockworkers taking breakfast. Arthur Hall, Jacob was deeply grateful to note, was nowhere to be seen. Instead, his customary spot behind the counter was taken by a thick-set old woman with a hunched back, beady eyes and silver hair tied in a bun. She was licking her thumb and using it to clean a mark off a spoon.

Jacob apprised his fellow inquisitor of everything that had happened, in as much detail as he could muster. When he reached the encounter with the innkeeper, she shook her head in disbelief.

"We must have him arrested," she told him firmly.

"On what charge?" he replied. "Anyway, 'tis my word against his."

"You are Master Pepys's personal inqu…"

"Aye, I told Arthur the same," he interjected. "He was not cowed by it."

"But…"

"Nay," said Jacob, taking her hand across the table. "I know how these dockyard men work. To take the matter further would be folly. I beseech you, do not mention it again."

His eyes implored her and she sighed. "Very well, Jacob."

He pulled his hand away. "Good," he said, smiling. "Now let us catch this Plague Doctor."

"Show me the note he dropped."

He passed it to her. "You recognise the hand?"

She peered at the writing. "I couldn't say for certain, but it does resemble…"

"The labels at Lydia Mercer's Plague Museum?"

"We shall have to revisit to be certain."

"Or confront the woman herself." He took the note back. "What can it mean? Who is the 'H' to whom it is addressed?"

"Hugo Hedges? Arthur Hall?" Abby mused. "You say Hall was here, awaiting you, when you returned from the Great Storehouse?"

"Aye, and sweaty he was, too."

"You think he may have been the Plague Doctor, returned here before you?"

"I cannot discern another reason for such sweating at two of the clock in the morning."

Abby was about to suggest one, when they were interrupted by the new serving woman. She was standing beside their table, tapping her foot impatiently. As wide as she was tall - about five-foot, Jacob estimated - she carried an air of distinct menace for one so old and of the supposedly fairer sex.

Abby imagined the old woman could handle herself, even among the Ship's loutish patrons, and her square features looked familiar. "Are you…?"

"Aye, I'm Arthur's mother," the old woman snarled. "You wish to make something of it?"

The inquisitors assured her they did not, which seemed to placate her.

"Breakfast's porridge," she barked.

"With honey?" Jacob asked hopefully.

Mistress Hall turned to leave, brutally expelling wind as she did so. "Prunes," she told him.

Shaken, Abby and Jacob returned to their deductions.

He prodded at the note. "This part, I believe I understand," he said. "'At midwatch' is a seafarer's term. It refers to the watchman's shift aboard ship, betwixt the hours of midnight and four of the clock."

"You encountered the Plague Doctor at which hour?"

"The church bell rang two of the clock not long afterwards."

She slapped the table. "This note summoned him, Jacob! 'Request visit from the crow…' A crow is black and associated with death. 'Tis the Plague Doctor, visiting between the hours of midnight and four!"

"Then 'Neptune's chariot' refers to a ship! Moreover, *The Ship*!"

"Which only leaves…"

Mistress Hall slammed Jacob's porridge down so force-fully, it erupted like a volcano and a lump landed on the end of his nose. He stared at it, cross-eyed, then at the innkeeper's mother. Fixing Jacob with a look that dared him to stop her, she leaned in, picked it off and ate it.

"Happy?" she asked, glaring.

"The woman has no genuine concern for my welfare," Jacob hissed when she had left.

Abby was intent upon deciphering the final portion of the coded message: 'Our friend of the watcher.'

"I have it!" she exclaimed suddenly. "Somebody who watches might equally be somebody who peeps! *Our friend of Mr Pepys!*"

Swarthy men in the vicinity were staring at her, she noticed. Grinning benignly at the nearest one, who was missing half an ear, Abby turned back to Jacob and told him in a hushed tone. "We have it, Jacob. Whoever wrote this note…"

"Lydia Mercer."

"*Whoever wrote this note* requested that the Plague Doctor, whose name begins with the letter H, visit you at this inn 'twixt the hours of midnight and four of the clock."

Jacob nodded emphatically.

But she was not finished. "Then why did he not harm you?"

The inquisitors puzzled some more over the identity of the mysterious 'H'. Both Hedges and Hall had good reason to wish Drake and Wilkes dead; however, the latter was only too aware that Jacob was staying at The Ship. Surely Hedges would also have known, Abby pointed out, in such a tight-knit community where they were undoubtedly the source of much gossip?

It left them with a murderer they were yet unacquainted with, who had passed up the opportunity to murder.

They concocted a plan. Most urgently, they should confront Lydia with the note to ascertain whether it was indeed penned by her hand. There was also the curious matter of the symbols inked behind the ears of both Kitty Blake and Arthur Bradshaw, assuming Jacob had not been mistaken. (He assured her he had not.)

The last time they spoke to Kitty, she had made it clear that she had revealed all she was willing to share. Although they were equally convinced the weasel Bradshaw would admit nothing, the inquisitors reasoned that visiting his place of work might throw up some clues.

As they were preparing to leave, Arthur Hall appeared in the doorway behind the counter, scanned the room, noticed the inquisitors and turned, hastily manhandling a figure behind him away from view. He was too late: Jacob had already spotted the glint of a jewelled headscarf and kicked Abby under the table. "Kitty Blake was with Hall!" he hissed.

"Last night?"

"I would wager as much, if they are seen together at this early hour."

"Kitty and Arthur, romantically entwined?" Abby mused, twirling a long strand of her red hair around her finger.

Chapter Twenty

Fresh Meat

Jacob tugged at Abby's sleeve. "Promise me that we will never again breakfast in The Ship," he urged her. "Hall's mother is mad."

"I rather like her," Abby replied. "She knows her own mind."

They were heading towards the market square and the Mercer & Sons chandlery. As they passed the end of Robert Drake's road, Abby suggested they divert and pay the purser a visit, since they were so close. "We've not seen him since the attempt on his life," she pointed out.

The previous day's rain had returned; even the gulls were silent, sheltering in the eaves of the dockyard buildings. No amount of foul weather would halt the relentless toil of the shipbuilders, yet Abby and Jacob found their ears were becoming used to the constant clamour, filtering it out as they did London's urban bustle.

When shortly they reached Drake's house, Jacob knocked. No one answered, and no sound came from within.

He tried again, louder.

The door to a neighbouring house opened, and a young woman appeared. "They've gone," she said.

Jacob removed his hat. "Gone?"

"Aye. After that Plague Doctor shot at him, killing poor Mr Catchpole. He took his wife and left."

"Do you know where they went?" Abby asked.

"To his father's, I was told, somewhere in the city."

It was proving to be a frustrating morning.

The market looked an altogether dreary prospect amid the wind and rain. Traders with uncovered stalls had erected awnings, and the crowd of shoppers sported an array of protective clothing of varying efficiency: hooded woollen cloaks, wide-brimmed hats and waxed capes.

But, oh, the wafting smells were still so good. The yeasty aroma of newly baked bread; an exotic note from imported spices; the freshness of newly cut herbs.

"Shall we have a pie?" Jacob asked, even though they had only just eaten.

"Nay, Mr Standish!" Abby scolded him. "Our time is precious."

Lydia Mercer was serving in her chandlery and hung her head when the inquisitors entered. "What do you want now?" she demanded, her tone heavy with exasperation.

Jacob pushed the note across the counter to her. "Did you pen this?"

"Nay," she said, without looking at it, and pushed it back.

"Please look at it, Lydia," said Abby.

Curiosity getting the better of her, the chandler reached for the note. As she read it, her expression darkened.

"What is it?" asked Abby.

Lydia stared at the paper incredulously. "What trickery is this?"

"What do you mean?" Abby asked.

"I did not pen this, yet it is in my hand."

Jacob snorted.

"I swear it!" Lydia exclaimed, crossing herself. "This note is forged!"

Jacob shook his head dismissively. "A likely tale! How is that even possible?"

Flustered, the chandler studied the handwriting as if willing it to supply the answer. "What if... What if the forger copied labels from my Plague Museum? Every letter of the alphabet is there, penned in my own hand..."

"Then who is 'H'?" Abby asked. "If the forger...," she ignored Jacob's loud splutter, "...took such great care over the hand, I assume they're aware you know this 'H'."

Lydia pinched her lower lip pensively. "Hugo Hedges?"

"Nay," Abby replied. "He surely knew Jacob was sleeping at The Ship. This 'H', we believe, is somebody unaware of our presence here in Deptford, yet once acquainted with you."

A black look crossed Lydia Mercer's haggard face. "It cannot be him," she muttered to herself.

"It cannot be who?" Abby asked.

Lydia crossed herself. "The Devil himself."

"Who?" urged Jacob, now fully engaged.

The whites of Lydia's eyes had turned bloodshot-red. "Henry Trevelyan."

The inquisitors looked at one another, perplexed. It was a name they had not heard before.

"Who is this Trevelyan?" Abby asked.

Lydia was in a daze. "A naval officer. He was the man I treated when I was a plague doctor," she said quietly, reliving the moment. "The one who blames me for the quack surgeon's amputation. If he is at large in Deptford, then my life is imperilled. I would never have penned such a note to him."

With gentle probing, the inquisitors were able to coax a fuller tale from her.

Following Trevelyan's amputation, which she had opposed, Lydia explained that his life had hung in the balance. "I confess I hoped secretly he would perish, since I was certain he would blame me for his disfigurement," she said. "Yet I was bound by a moral duty to care for the afflicted, and so I continued to minister to him. Until his consciousness returned. Then I fled."

She found herself in hiding, Lydia explained, both from Trevelyan and from the wider dockyard populace, having been unmasked as an unqualified woman treating people's sick loved ones.

Then she had a stroke of luck. "Trevelyan, I discovered, was on the run from the Admiralty. Somebody must have tipped them off, since one night his hiding place was found and he was arrested. When he was jailed, I breathed a sigh of relief." She paused. "Yet this note concerns me. Is he now returned for his revenge?"

"Did you tip off the Admiralty?" Jacob asked.

Lydia shook her head vigorously. "I would never have dared. Anyway I had no need. A man makes many enemies cooped up at sea."

Chapter Twenty-One

Turning Bad

*H*enry Trevelyan was delighted when the Dutch war dragged on for another two years, following his celebrated heroics at the Battle of Kentish Knock. As a newly promoted captain in charge of the Venturer, he played his part in a number of feted actions, most notably the Battle of Portland, in which his old mentor, Robert Blake, was seriously wounded yet survived.

The war culminated in the Battle of Scheveningen in the summer of 1653. There, off the coast of Holland, 2,000 Dutchmen were slain, including their supreme commander, Maarten Tromp, and their demoralised fleet routed. The Venturer had been just one of the chasing pack.

Despite the pride that Henry took in fighting for his country – and winning, naturally – he found himself unable to garner the attention he craved. Being Captain, though he had dreamed of attaining the rank since joining the navy, demanded too much responsibility. He could hardly abandon his own ship to

race off on some foolhardy yet ultimately brilliant counter-at-
tack.

He also discovered that the men now gave him a wide berth.
As a lieutenant, he had been one of them: someone to look up
to, yet on their side. A leader and a colleague. As the Captain,
he occupied a higher station altogether, one the lower ranks
respected and feared.

There were other issues. These men he was charged to
command were a motley crew. Many had been press-ganged
into service in England by men who cared little for their
suitability to the task, merely that they made up the numbers.
How was he supposed to turn a desk clerk with the temerity
of a child into a seafaring man of action?

Then there was the pay. While he was at sea, he had been
promised the monthly wage of 16 pounds. Sometimes, he was
paid; other times, he was offered excuses. Henry had acquired
expensive tastes, as befitted his status: exotic-wood furniture,
gold and silver jewellery, fine wines of distinction, tobacco of
the highest quality... How was he supposed to afford all these
luxuries, so richly deserved, if the navy did not pay him?

And so he grew disaffected.

When, in 1662, King Charles married the Portuguese
princess, Catherine of Braganza, part of his dowry was the
port of Tangier, then occupied by Portugal. Royal Navy ships
were required to carry men and supplies to the new outpost,
and Henry immediately committed the Venturer to the fleet.

At last, *he thought,* a chance to escape this rut in the cause of vengeance.

He was thinking only of his father, Thomas, who had been kidnapped by corsairs all those years ago. Corsairs - from the Barbary coast: an area that included Morocco, the mother country of Tangier.

He had no idea whether the corsairs he so dearly sought were in fact from Algiers, Tunis, or Tripoli, elsewhere along the Barbary coast. All he cared about was finally having a chance to act. He would track down those cowards who had hunted in a pack to capture the lone Cornish fisherman, with no regard for that man's son. He would punish them and rescue his father.

It did not work out like that. All of Henry Trevelyan's fanciful bravado was reduced to a stark reality when the Venturer sailed past the coast of North Africa. The area the corsairs operated from was vast. He had no chance of tracking down the men responsible for the kidnapping, he quickly realised, and still less chance of finding his father. It was a pointless endeavour.

Which did not stop him from trying. Pinning all his hopes on his father having been taken to Tangier, Henry scoured the city. He toured the marketplaces, bars, streets and the Kasbah. He befriended English merchants who had captured corsair vessels. He sought contacts among the locals, asking after the broad-shouldered Cornishman with green eyes and sandy hair - the spit of himself - who had been enslaved in North Africa some 30 years ago.

He was met with blank faces. Henry never found a trace of his father. But he did find Katherina Al-Yazid, and she entranced him.

Henry had never married. The sea was his mistress; she was in his bones. Even when the light dimmed on his naval career, he still found fortitude and purpose in life afloat. When the storms came and the Venturer was flung about like God's own plaything, when it looked as if all aboard might perish, that was when he came alive.

Katherina changed all that. Those eyes. When he gazed into them, he was rapt, transported to faraway lands, accompanied by the song of sirens. When he fell into her arms, he melted into her smooth, golden skin and became one with her, lost in a world that might well have been Heaven. He fell hopelessly in love.

She was no fool, either. When Henry moaned to her about his irregular pay, it was she who suggested the sideline in smuggling. A barrel of valuable contraband, here or there among the Venturer's other hundreds of barrels? What harm could it do? He had earned it.

Katherina set up the unwritten smuggling contract for him, using her contacts in Tangier, and the plan worked. A cut for her, the rest for him and his accomplices. Easy money, far and above what the navy paid. Afterwards, he made sure the Venturer was always the first ship his employers called upon when a Tangier trip was due.

Then, one day in the late spring of 1665, when he was back in Africa, he found her with tears in her eyes. Her parents had arranged a marriage for her, she told him, to a rival merchant's son. It would trap her in a life of drudgery and servitude, far removed from the legal hustles and shady dealings she was accustomed to.

"Take me back to England with you," she implored him.

He was powerless to refuse.

It would be his undoing.

The omens for the return journey looked ill from the moment the Venturer set off. A glowing ball of light was spotted in the night sky, with a long tail, travelling east. Some aboard saw it as a sign from God that their return journey was blessed. Others feared that it predicted a disaster of some kind – a battle lost or a sickness aboard. Either way, it unsettled the crew.

When news reached Henry's ears that a mutiny was brewing over the lack of regular wages, he knew he had to act quickly and decisively. And he did so, handing out 36 lashes to each man found guilty, in front of their crew-mates.

In the aftermath, one of his crew chanced upon Kitty's hiding place and threatened to inform the Admiralty that he had allowed a stowaway aboard one of the King's ships.

The mental turmoil skewed his thoughts and made him act irrationally. Is this how it ends? *he wondered to himself.* After all those years of dedicated service to the King and the Commonwealth? Cast out of the navy, purely because I am in love with the woman secreted deep in the hold of this vessel?

It would ruin him, he knew, but he surrendered to the blackmail to keep his lover hidden. His entire share of the spoils from their smuggling operation was to be the cost.

The Venturer made it back to Deptford, and Henry was able to smuggle Kitty away into the safety of the town, yet he could not just forgive the blackmail. The disloyalty of this man who had dared threaten his liberty – a blackguard he was worth ten of – ate away at him, and he made plans to dispatch the despicable rogue.

Two events occurred that would seal his fate. Talk of his murderous plan found its way among the loose-tongued patrons of his local inn, The Ship; and he fell ill with a fever that so debilitated him, he feared he would not survive it.

One day, or night – he did not know, so suffused with delirium had his mind become – he became aware of an intense pain and awoke screaming. When he opened his eyes, there before him was a vision of such madness that he felt certain he must be imagining it. Clawing at the vision in a state of pure dementia, he noticed with horror that one of his hands was missing, and with the other he was holding some sort of unholy bird-mask. Among all that was a woman's face, frozen in terror, with orange hair like flames . . .

Then he passed out.

Henry had no idea how long he lay unconscious. He drifted in and out of wakefulness, moaning and feverish, aware only vaguely that somebody was mopping his brow or pouring cool liquid into his mouth, which he felt drip over his cheek and run down his neck.

Very gradually, his mind began to clear, and the house in which he was resting took solid form. As did the face of the guardian angel who was nursing him back to health. He recognised it as Lydia Mercer's, the chandler's wife. Although he tried to thank her, his mind was still so fogged that the words would not come.

His wrist, where his left hand had been, was bandaged tightly. Somehow - pure bloody-mindedness, Henry felt sure, passed on by his father - he survived the ordeal.

By the time he was fully recovered, Lydia was nowhere to be seen, and his thoughts turned to tracking down the blackmailer and avenging his treachery. That was when the soldiers came. The agents of the Admiralty kicked down the door and hauled him to his feet.

"Henry Trevelyan," their leader said. "You are to be court-martialled for knowingly harbouring a stowaway aboard one of the King's ships. Take him away."

The blackmailer had found him first.

Found guilty, based on his previous impeccable service, he was sentenced leniently to six months in jail. However, all his earthly goods were forfeit - no doubt sold to pay sailors' wages from the King's purse, *Henry thought to himself wryly - and he was forced to go underground on his release.*

He had become acquainted with all manner of men in Newgate jail, known for housing traitors, rebels and heretics. He made contacts there with people who knew people who would pay a man handsomely to do their criminal bidding. It suited him fine. He would earn himself a crust, then return to Deptford for his one true love – and for his revenge.

The proud Cornish fisherman's heart had become blackened.

Chapter Twenty-Two

The Warehouse

Abby and Jacob were directed to Peter Bradshaw's warehouse by a dockworker. When they arrived there, they were stunned to find that it was a building they had already encountered. Bradshaw's place of work was one of the very tall, two-storey buildings that overshadowed Lydia Mercer's Plague Museum. The two prime suspects were neighbours.

"It explains why we saw Bradshaw pass us when first we visited," said Abby.

"It also places Bradshaw merely yards from the plague-doctor garb in the museum," Jacob pointed out. "The same garb that we believe was donned by the murderer."

"While we're here, we should ensure it hasn't been moved," she said.

At the rear of the Plague Museum, they discovered the door unlocked, as they had left it. Inside, the blanket was still strewn across the floor, and the plague-doctor mask eyed them, unseeing, from its place beneath the long robe on the floor. It was eerily reassuring.

As they left, they became aware of the deep, raucous sound of sawing. A large nearby trench, previously empty, Jacob now noticed was a saw-pit. A 'sawyer' was standing on top of an immense log, holding one end of a long saw, while his colleague, hidden inside the trench, held the other. They pulled and pushed in unison, cutting the timber methodically down the middle. To Jacob, it had always looked like back-breaking, intensive labour, and he felt glad again to have left behind the drudgery of the dockyard.

The old sawyer caught Jacob staring at him and stopped what he was doing. His clothing was ripped and poorly patched, and his back was hideously stooped. "Do I know you?" he called out.

When Jacob said nothing, he added, "You were at Woolwich dockyard? Apprentice purser?"

Abby saw that Jacob was furiously adjusting his periwig.

"Slackjaw Jake!" the sawyer exclaimed. "Slackjaw Jake, who sent the men to sea with a thimble of ale!"

The sawyer's hidden partner sniggered, the mocking sound echoing from within the deep pit.

A haunted look crossed Jacob's face. Abby tugged on his sleeve, which shook him from his trance, and she dragged him away, around the side of the Plague Museum.

"'Tis a shame they know nought of your esteemed position as Mr Samuel Pepys's personal inquisitor," Abby told him as they negotiated the alleyway between Bradshaw's warehouse and the museum.

But Jacob was not for appeasing. "Slackjaw Jake, who sent the men to sea with a thimble of ale," he muttered to himself, remembering. "That is how they taunted me."

"Who taunted you?" Abby asked.

"All of them," Jacob replied quietly. "All of them, once word spread."

Abby stopped and took him by the forearms, staring until he returned her gaze. All they could hear was the rhythmic scything of the saw. "The men of the dockyard are swill-bellies and thugs, Jacob. Pay them no heed."

He closed his eyes. "I shall never escape my past."

She shook him. "You *have* escaped your past, Mr Standish! Look at you! An inquisitor, who saved Master Pepys's sister from the hangman's noose, and he was most grateful and proud!"

One of his eyes opened, and he squinted at her. "I did save Paulina, did I not?"

Grinning, she took him by the hand and they continued on their way.

"Deptford celebrates! Mr Pepys's interlopers return!" came the derisive call.

Peter Bradshaw was staring at them from the end of the alleyway, clapping slowly as the inquisitors approached.

"We wish to visit your warehouse, Mr Bradshaw," Abby told him when they were face-to-face.

"I am open to all," Bradshaw replied, sweeping his arm in a grand, condescending gesture of welcome.

He led the way along the waterfront towards his warehouse entrance. Jacob surreptitiously pointed out to Abby the small blue, inked rabbit just visible behind his left ear. *Now what*, she wondered, *are the chances of Bradshaw explaining the symbol's origins, and his connection to Kitty Blake?*

As they followed Bradshaw, the inquisitors, both well-acquainted with Thames traffic from their previous experiences, were still struck by its sheer magnitude. That afternoon, with a high tide incoming, an even greater number of vessels seemed to be taking advantage of the powerful wash upriver.

Galleons mingled with lighters, barges with yawls, and wherries navigated between them all, ferrying travellers from one place to another. The inquisitors marvelled at the massed masts of the passing vessels. They heard the creak of timber, the rhythmic lapping of the river against the embankment, and the cries of sailors. And amidst it all, the constant, reassuring background clamour of Deptford's dockyard thrumming with activity.

Truly, the Thames is a microcosm of life itself, Abby thought to herself. She had become fascinated by the river when she lived with relatives in Greenwich, and had made it her business to learn of its ways.

Almost a quarter of all Londoners depended on the Thames for their livelihoods, she recalled reading. Besides the steady flow of coal shipments from Newcastle to satisfy London's ever-growing demand, and the transport of essential goods and foodstuffs from around Britain's coastline, recent decades had seen England emerge as a leader in trade across the known world.

Timber from Norway and the Baltic; silks from Turkey; Italian rice and oil; salt and cinnamon from Portugal; Spanish wine, fruit and tobacco; wool from the Bay of Biscay... Much of it was not even consumed within England, the re-export market having lately burgeoned; merchants merely stored their imported wares on home soil before shipping them out to buyers abroad. Most popular of all re-export goods was sugar, from the Caribbean and other hot climes, a trade in which London led the way.

These were lucrative times, Abby knew. *No doubt, Peter Bradshaw is aware of the same,* she mused.

The sign on his warehouse door read:

P BRADSHAW – WAREHOUSING
H HEDGES – MERCHANT

Not just firm friends, it seemed that the pair were linked in business, too.

Inside, the ceiling was higher than any Abby had seen outside of a church. Jacob, who had visited the Great Storehouse itself, was only mildly less impressed. The space stretched as far as the eye could see, filled with barrel after barrel and crate after crate.

Shafts of daylight streamed in through the windows around the timber walls. The space was filled with a medley of scents, exotic and mundane, so numerous that Abby could not discern any one in particular.

"How may I assist you?" It was Hugo Hedges, leaning on a long sales counter to the right of the entrance.

Abby strolled towards him. "By showing me the symbol inked behind your left ear," she said. It was a shot in the dark.

Self-consciously, the merchant pulled his feathered hat tightly down over his head.

Abby smiled. "I'll assume there is one. Pray, what is its significance?"

Bradshaw interjected on his business partner's behalf. "Its significance," he replied, bending so that his steely grey eyes were level with hers, "is that those who enquire of it place themselves in grave danger."

Jacob had been inspecting the stored goods and was standing among a series of bulging animal bladders used to contain paint. "I see that you stock black paint, Mr

Bradshaw," he called across. "Have you painted any crosses on doors lately, perchance?"

The warehouse owner let out a filthy, throaty laugh and threw his arm around Hedges, who was looking distinctly uncomfortable. "I admire your pluck, Samuel Pepys's inquisitors. However I would advise you to desist and toddle off back to your fine houses in the city. You do not understand the ways of the sea and are likely to be drowned."

"Lydia Mercer told us of a Henry Trevelyan, of whom she is greatly afeared," Abby said. "Do you know this man?"

Bradshaw and Hedges shared a glance, and the rat-faced merchant fingered his cutlass. Jacob moved in to protect Abby, and she acknowledged his presence with a tight smile.

Hedges broken the tension with a sigh. "Henry Trevelyan is a legendary naval captain whom we had the pleasure and privilege to serve under," he explained in a conciliatory tone. "He has not been seen in Deptford in many a moon. Word on the docks is he became an assassin for hire."

"Then he may be the Plague Doctor?" Jacob asked.

Hedges looked to Bradshaw, who remained impassive.

Abby suddenly clutched her temples. "I have it!" she exclaimed. "Lydia Mercer's naval officer, Henry Trevelyan, and Kitty Blake's English sea captain, Henry - they are one and the same. Thus you all sailed from Tangier on the Venturer together!"

She needed no confirmation.

Chapter Twenty-Three

Cloak & Dagger

When the inquisitors arrived at The Ship, it was customarily full, if unusually quiet. Arthur Hall was in his usual spot, cleaning cutlery with a rag dirtier than the utensils themselves. When he saw Jacob, his expression was blank, as if their fearful encounter in the gambling den had never taken place.

The tables were largely occupied, and they spotted Kitty Blake seated towards the rear of the tap-room, near the place where she sang. She was accompanied by a stranger - which was not unusual - in a long, black cloak and a wide-brimmed hat of the same colour. He wore a red linen kerchief around his neck, and the hair protruding beneath his hat was sandy-coloured.

They appeared deep in conversation, and the inn's patrons occasionally cast them wary glances. The atmosphere was taut.

"Who's that with Kitty?" Abby asked Jacob, as they commandeered a spare table.

He turned around to look. "I know not," he replied. "What shall we eat? I am gut-foundered."

"You're always hungry," she chided him.

As she did so, she saw Arthur deliver two tankards to Kitty's table. The cloaked stranger stood, grabbed the innkeeper by the scruff of the neck, and launched him into the wall behind, sending ale flying in arcs.

While all eyes fixed on the scene, no one moved to intervene.

From beneath his cloak, the stranger drew a pistol and pointed it at the innkeeper, who was pushing himself to his feet. "While I am incarcerated, detained at His Majesty's pleasure, you steal my woman from me, Arthur Hall!" he said.

Hardly a man to be easily cowed, the innkeeper wiped ale from his face and snarled back, "Who says she is yours to keep, Henry Trevelyan?"

The inquisitors' eyes widened. Kitty leapt up and tried to pull Henry away, but he pushed her away and she sprawled to the floor.

Abby grabbed Jacob's shoulder. "Look! He has a hook for a hand!"

In that instant, Arthur took his chance and lunged at Henry, who fired his pistol. It caught the innkeeper in the shoulder, and he was thrown backwards against the wall. Replacing the single-shot weapon in his belt, Henry pulled Kitty to her feet and kissed her on the lips.

"I shall return for you later, my sweet," he told her, producing an ivory-handled knife from beneath the cloak.

Waving it in front of him, he began making his way out of the inn.

When Jacob moved to confront him, Henry pointed the tip of the blade in the direction of the inquisitor's heart. "The first man who tries to stop me dies!"

"Let him go, Jacob," Abby urged.

"Aye, let him go, Jacob," Henry echoed her.

No man barred his way, and with a waft of his cloak he was gone.

Abby spoke urgently. "Remember our earliest case, concerning Master Pepys's stolen diaries?"

"Aye, naturally," Jacob replied. After all, they had only solved it a fortnight ago, even if the intensity of the intervening period had made it feel like half a lifetime. "You believe that Henry Trevelyan may also be 'Hook-Hand'? Surely there is many a sailor who has lost a limb to a cannonball or a cutlass?"

Abby regarded him with her piercing turquoise eyes. "My instinct says 'tis the same man, Jacob."

Chapter Twenty-Four

Surprise!

Arthur Hall was fortunate that the musket ball had passed cleanly through his shoulder, greatly reducing the risk of infection. He shrugged off Kitty Blake's urging to visit the hospital; instead, he bandaged himself up and continued with his work undaunted.

"Sing!" he ordered her, and she obeyed.

The inn returned to its semblance of normal.

Having dispatched her supper, Abby was tucking into a dish of stewed pears with custard sauce. "Hall is built like one of the King's galleons," she said to Jacob. "I would not wish to fight with him."

"I would rather fight Hall than his mother," he replied. "And what of Henry Trevelyan?"

"Hook-Hand, you mean."

"It was you who told me that only the fool speculates," Jacob pointed out, stabbing at his apple fritters with a spoon.

She stilled him with her hand. "Trust me, Jacob. Trevelyan is Hook-Hand. I would lay money on it."

"You have no money!" he pointed out, then apologised for his bluntness.

Abby set out their recent discoveries. That Bradshaw and Hall had sailed from Tangier aboard a ship, the Venturer, captained by Henry Trevelyan. That the Captain had stowed away Kitty Blake aboard the same vessel. And that Bradshaw, Blake and, they assumed, Hedges had a symbol inked behind their left ears. It linked them somehow. "We must discover the link," she said.

They knew also that Henry Trevelyan, so feared by Lydia Mercer, had turned up in Deptford for some unknown reason. Had he been there all along, hiding? Was he the Plague Doctor? Where was he now, and when would he reappear?

"He told Kitty that he would return for her, so we must be on our guard," said Jacob. Scraping up the last of his custard with his spoon, he swallowed it with a flourish. Tapping the table thoughtfully, he added, "I have not asked you about the foreign words you spoke with Kitty Blake yesterday. What language was that? It was not Greek or Latin, in which I am... somewhat versed, having been tutored in them at Oxford. Was it...?"

"It was French, Jacob," she told him. "Master Pepys's wife, Elizabeth, speaks it fluently. Her father was French and she was schooled in Paris. Master Pepys, being infinitely curious, studies the language himself."

"He allows you to accompany him?"

"We study together on occasion. It makes the process more enjoyable, he says. I am but an amateur."

"What did you say to Kitty?"

Abby looked at him blankly.

"It concerned…" Jacob squinted, stroking his stubbly chin. "The bow pays of a mond?"

She laughed. "*Les beaux pays de la monde.* The beautiful countries of the world. I told her I wished to visit them."

"Which ones?"

"Any, Mr Standish. Do you not wish to explore the world beyond your doorstep?"

Jacob shrugged. "I once sailed to Holland with the navy and found the people most uncivil."

Abby flung up her hands in exasperation. "I would die for the chance!"

"Then we must pray that is not necessary." The familiar voice came from a figure arriving at their table.

Abby gasped and covered her mouth with her hand.

"Mr Pepys!" Jacob exclaimed, rising to his feet and bowing.

Having gathered her wits, Abby stood also. "Master Pepys," she intoned, bowing also.

Impatiently, Pepys motioned for them to be seated and pulled up a stool for himself. Removing his hat, he shook rain from it, which cascaded over the floor. "The weather has turned most foul," he said, just as a loud crash of thunder announced itself. "Arthur!" he called out.

As if by magic, the innkeeper appeared beside him, bowing deeply. "Mr Pepys, 'tis always my pleasure to welcome such an esteemed gentleman to my humble establishment. How may I assist you, sir?"

Pepys looked towards Abby and Jacob, who had been rendered mute by the innkeeper's bewildering politeness. "Three half-pints of sack," he said abruptly, ordering the fortified white wine on their behalf.

The innkeeper retreated backward, bowing. "It will be my pleasure, sir."

Abby stifled a smirk.

"What brings you to Deptford, sir?" asked Jacob.

"All in good time, Mr Standish," Pepys replied. "First you must apprise me of your news. I am eager to hear it."

Abby noticed her master attracting furtive glances and hushed conversations among the seated dockworkers. Pepys was certainly not shy of announcing his high status; his rich burgundy velvet coat was embroidered with gold thread, and his silk stockings alone, which shimmered in the inn's candlelight, were worth a dozen of the tatty outfits worn by the impoverished workers thereabouts.

Jacob, in particular, could not help envying his mentor's intricately curled chestnut-brown periwig, which smelled, even at a distance, of exquisitely scented powders. Although Pepys's was drenched in rain, it still held its fine shape, unlike Jacob's, which drooped from his head like an exhausted dog. He found himself primping his periwig uselessly.

Having been updated on the inquisitors' investigation, Pepys reached into a leather bag embossed with his initials, pulled out a hefty, rectangular ledger and opened it on the table.

The innkeeper arrived, carrying three pewter goblets, and set them down beside the ledger.

Abby picked one up and inspected it. "This rim is filthy," she said.

Arthur's eyeballs seemed to pulsate, and he clenched his massive fists. As he opened his mouth to reply, Pepys interjected, "Indeed, it is. Change it, would you?"

Instantly, the fists relaxed, and the innkeeper's obsequious alter-ego returned. "Certainly, Mr Pepys. At once, Mr Pepys. I do beg your pardon." He snatched the goblet from Abby, eyeing her evilly, and retreated, bowing.

"Do not antagonise him, Abigail. I forbid it," Pepys chastised her. "He is a decent man, if at times disconcerting."

Jacob realised he had been holding his breath. "Sir, we heard tell that Arthur Hall stole from the East India Company, for whom he worked, and sold the spoils on the black market. For which he was justly punished."

Pepys licked his index finger and began flicking through the ledger's thick pages. Without looking up, he replied, "Prior to his becoming innkeeper of this fine establishment, Arthur Hall was a gardener of some renown, who was employed in the art of topiary and suchlike by the Vicar of Deptford."

Both inquisitors shuffled uncomfortably on their stools.

Pepys went on, "As I have discovered among seafaring folk, Mr Standish, it is vital to discern in whom to place one's trust." Alighting upon a particular entry in the ledger, he suddenly prodded the paper angrily. "Here," he snapped. "A discrepancy." Rifling a few pages back, he prodded again. "And here." Repeating the process, he concluded, "And here. There are others, dating back to 1664. What do you make of it, Mr Standish?"

Although Jacob had been trained in the practice of accounting and stock-taking as an apprentice purser at Woolwich dockyard, he had never really come to grips with the process. Figures were not his strength; they swam before his eyes.

Realising that flattery was the better part of honesty, Jacob replied, "Sir, you are the expert in this field, and I would respectfully value your opinion over mine."

Pepys could not disguise a flicker of smugness. "As you wish, Mr Standish. See here, the recorded weights of these barrels of gunpowder do not tally. According to the figure recorded by the ship's purser, each barrel did weigh

100 pounds. Now see here..." Pepys flicked over the page and stabbed at it with his finger. "Yet the Collector of Customs did record the same barrel as weighing 300 pounds. A blatant discrepancy, and it appears I am the first to notice."

Pepys explained that he had felt useless sitting in his office on Seething Lane, distractedly awaiting news from his inquisitors, so began an investigation of his own. Digging out the Deptford dockyard ledgers, he had methodically pored over each one, seeking out any inconsistencies.

Only when he reached the records of one particular vessel, near the bottom of his tottering pile of ledgers, were his suspicions fully aroused.

"Was that vessel the Venturer, Master Pepys?" Abby asked.

Pepys sat back, eyes widened. "Aye, Abigail, it was. I am most impressed," he replied, snapping the book shut. "Captained by one Henry Trevelyan. A rum scoundrel, if ever there were one."

Chapter Twenty-Five

The Venturer

The three of them discussed Pepys's findings.

The weight of certain barrels, he assured them, had been falsely recorded by the purser aboard the Venturer. When the Customs officer checked the same barrels after they had been unloaded at Deptford, they weighed three times as much. Something did not add up.

Pepys had discovered the ship's purser to be none other than Robert Drake.

"Fie, sir!" Jacob exclaimed. "The very man we seek to protect from the Plague Doctor!"

Pepys shook his head. "It makes no sense, Mr Standish. I have worked with Drake and have always found him to be upstanding and trustworthy. We may discover that he has been coerced by way of violence, or even blackmailed, by the scoundrel, Trevelyan, or by a member of his dastardly gang, to enter these false records. There is skullduggery at work, mark my words."

"Sir, we saw Trevelyan but one hour ago, in this very hostelry."

Pepys choked on his sack. "Here? An hour past?" he spluttered. "But the blackguard was jailed."

Jacob recounted the fight with the innkeeper, and Pepys saw that Hall's shoulder was indeed wrapped in a bloodied bandage.

Abby spoke up. "Sir, we believe that Trevelyan may have started the fire that lately levelled the city of London. We encountered him when we investigated your stolen diaries, though we knew him only as 'Hook-Hand' since he…"

Pepys cupped his hands over his ears. "I will hear no more of it, Abigail Harcourt! Truly, you do astonish me! Will you next accuse me of lighting the fire myself?"

"Sir, if I might add," said Jacob, "I did not believe…"

Hushing him, Pepys turned again on Abby. "It is well known that the fire was started at the bakery of Thomas Farriner of Pudding Lane, and that is how history will record it. Henry Trevelyan, indeed! A reprobate and a bilge-rat, he may be; a starter of fires, he is not."

Abby bowed her head.

"Where next, Mr Pepys?" Jacob asked.

"Why, to the Venturer, Mr Standish. She lies here in the King's Shipyard, as we speak."

"But, sir, it is late and…"

"And there is no time like the present!"

The weather outside was foul. Torrential rain lashed down, beating on the wood, thatch and stone dockyard surfaces, creating a constant drumming. Pepys and Jacob pushed their lanterns deep inside their heavy coats, protecting the flames from being extinguished. Abby lagged behind, silently brooding. The three of them were drenched in seconds, and the water ran in rivulets from the men's sagging felt hats.

Clouds concealed the moon and the stars. Deptford dockyard was darker and grimmer than ever.

"Sir, are you sure this...?" Jacob's voice trailed off as Pepys pressed on ahead.

Fortunately, the King's Shipyard lay opposite the inn, and their journey was mercifully brief. The inquisitors had become familiar with the sight of the two vast painted galleons docked there, little knowing that one of them would become so central to their investigation.

A long wooden ladder had been tethered alongside the Venturer's scaffolding, which led up to the main deck. Looking upwards from the foot of it, the ship's masts seemed to pierce the very heavens. To Abby, it was a daunting sight.

Even Pepys hesitated as he eyed the route upwards. Steeling himself, he mounted the first rung, shifting his leather sole on the slippery surface, testing its sturdiness. As satisfied as he could ever be, he began the climb.

Jacob looked down at Abby, her sodden garb cling-ing to her slight form, and took her hand. "Come," he said gently, ushering her towards the ladder. "You step first. I shall catch you, should you slip."

And so, tentatively, Pepys, then Abby, then Jacob, made their way up the side of the Venturer, the lad-der bouncing unnervingly with each footstep. The raindrops pounded their faces, and their cold hands gripped the rough wood until their knuckles whitened.

When Jacob guided Abby over the Venturer's wide gunwale, she felt so grateful she was close to tears. Stumbling onto the main deck, she flung herself at her fellow inquisitor and clung to him as if to life itself.

"Let us go below," Pepys urged. "Escape this pesti-lent weather."

"What do we seek, sir?" Jacob asked, blowing rain from his lips.

"We shall know when we find it, Mr Standish."

The substance of the vessel on which Abby was standing quickly allayed her fears, and she took in her surroundings. One of the masts had been erected, thick as an ancient oak, and she craned her neck to see the crow's nest at its top. She imagined a man climbing the rigging, to reach what amounted to an open lookout barrel some 50 feet above the deck, and shuddered involuntarily.

All around her, the dark timbers were bulkier than she had ever seen before. Coiled ropes resembled a giant's thread, and the iron cannon looked immovable. Everything felt so… solid. It made her feel safe, as if no earthly opponent could ever breach the sanctity of the Venturer.

Jacob's thoughts were swirling, also. He had experienced this before, many times, and the memories were not happy ones. Up ahead, he saw the forecastle, the forward deck; under there, he had slept - uneasily - among the ordinary seaman, who had shunned the cosseted son of the Navy Board's Surveyor. Cramped and stifled, crammed into his hammock between so many others, wishing he were anywhere else.

He saw the many hatches dotted about the deck, covered in wooden vents. It reminded him of the cries of, "Batten down the hatches!" When the storms came, sailors hurriedly sealed the vents with canvas, preventing great washes across the deck from flooding the ship. It was all coming back to him.

Turning, he noticed Mr Pepys's head disappear down a hatch, grabbed Abby's hand, and pulled her towards it.

The steps down were steep and narrow, and the inquisitors trod carefully. The light from Pepys's lantern awaited them at the bottom.

It was very dark on the gun deck. Timber creaked and the rain beat on the deck above. Abby fancied she caught the faint whiff of a ghost of gunpowder once ignited, from the cannons all around her.

The ceiling was low enough that Jacob removed his hat, just in case. "Mr Pepys, may I make a suggestion?"

Pepys, his round, ruddy face and eager eyes framed in golden, flickering candlelight, nodded.

"We know that the singer from Tangier, Kitty Blake, was stowed away in the hold, sir. Might we begin there?"

"A fine suggestion, Mr Standish," said Pepys. "Will you lead the way?"

It threw him briefly. He had never been aboard the Venturer; how would he know the route to the bowels of the vessel? Then it struck him: ship design had barely changed in the past century; the layout of one galleon would be similar enough to another's. Fired by his mentor's confidence in him, he set off, his lantern held straight out before him, a haze of yellow light in the intense darkness.

Past cannons and rows of hanging buckets, Jacob arrived quickly at the next flight down, leading to the Venturer's orlop deck. Deep in the belly of the vessel, sounds seemed muffled and the space felt claustrophobic.

Jacob shone his lantern around as he waited for his accomplices. The deck stretched further than the candlelight would reach. A line of thick, supporting wooden pillars disappeared into the gloom, accompanied by creaking of the timbers.

It was here, on the orlop deck, that the surgeon operated on wounded men, safely below the reach of incoming cannon-fire.

"Pray, continue, Mr Standish," Pepys said when he and Abby joined Jacob.

One final set of steps down, and the three of them found themselves in the hold, in the very depths of the Venturer. The entire space would ordinarily have been stacked to the rafters with crated provisions; since it was empty, Jacob assumed the ship was not due to set sail. He could hear the scurrying of rats.

Trusting his intuition, he led the way towards the stern, his footsteps echoing in the darkness. If somebody were hiding a stowaway, then the furthest corners would make perfect sense.

Out of the blackness, a large pile of barrels appeared, three high and perhaps fifteen wide – as wide as the stern itself. "Here," he stated firmly. "This must be the place."

"Why do you say that, Jacob?" Abby asked.

"Elsewhere is bare," he explained. "These barrels are here for a reason, which, I would suggest, is concealment."

His theory only grew in strength when he and Pepys, shifting the barrels to discover what was behind, found them to be empty. Yet, when they had all been moved aside, only a bare timber wall presented itself, made from horizontal planks and vertical struts.

Gazing at it, Jacob bit his lower lip.

"It does appear that you are mistaken, Mr Standish," Pepys remarked.

"Hold," said Abby, and she knocked on the wall.

All three of them pricked their ears. The resulting sound was neither as deep nor as deadened as they would have expected.

"Is it hollow?" She asked.

Jacob began inspecting the timbers, holding his lantern against the wood and peering closely. "Aha!" he exclaimed at length.

Pepys joined him, squinting through his ailing eyes. "What is it? What have you discovered?"

A large knot in the wood appeared to be covered in scratch-marks, as if it had been handled often. Easing the knot towards him, Jacob discovered it was easily removed. Hooking his index finger through the resulting hole, he tugged.

Nothing happened.

He tugged again, harder.

This time, a concealed door opened outward. When Jacob shone his light inside, a hiding space was revealed, perhaps five feet deep by 40 feet wide. Although it was empty, it was undoubtedly where Kitty Blake had stowed away.

Abby gasped.

Pepys slapped Jacob on the back. "Well done, sir!" he exclaimed delightedly. "Such a fine inquisitor, as I had always imagined would be the case!"

Thin shafts of light cast by Pepys's lantern outside the hideaway revealed ventilation holes hidden about the wall. Still, there were no windows, and the constant rolling of the ship would have made any journey experienced there exquisitely uncomfortable.

In the nearest corner was a folded sheet of canvas and an empty ale pot. Looking closer, Jacob spotted a few crumbs of bread crust in the crevices between floorboards.

"Poor Kitty," said Abby. "There is scant comfort here."

Jacob turned to her. "Yet this space is larger than she let on," he said. "Indeed, there would be room enough here for the woman and… several barrels?"

Abby and Pepys watched in an expectant hush as he crawled on his hands and knees, peering among the floorboards, towards the far end of the hideaway.

"Sir!" he suddenly exclaimed.

"What is it, Standish?" Pepys replied, hurrying to him.

"Taste this."

"What is it?"

"I found patches of it here on the floor. A dark brown grit, sir."

Jacob held some up in his palm. Pepys licked his fingertip, dabbed it onto the crystals, and, very cautiously, tasted them with the tip of his tongue.

"Sugar, Mr Standish!" he exclaimed. "Sugar!"

"Aye, sir," said Jacob. "A most expensive luxury, yet easily concealed. Perfect for smuggling."

Chapter Twenty-Six

A Letter

The church bell chimed the eleventh hour as Abby and Jacob returned to The Ship, drenched through and their teeth chattering. The inn's blazing fireplace instantly lifted their spirits.

Pepys had parted ways with them upon leaving the Venturer (a ladder descent Abby had not relished but which she accomplished with gritted teeth).

"There is an urgent errand, which only I am authorised to attend to," he had told them mysteriously, before scurrying off into the torrid Deptford night.

The Ship's tap-room was once again heaving with life, its tables all occupied. Seafarers and dockworkers had a great capacity for ale and revelry at all hours, the inquisitors were becoming aware.

Kitty Blake was in her usual spot, singing a song they did not recognise. Her boisterous audience, standing on tables and clanking their tankards together, joined in with the chorus, which went:

With a down, derry, derry, derry down, down!

"Where've you been snooping now?" Arthur Hall asked when they reached his counter and ordered drink. "Your precious master returned home, has he, tail 'twixt his legs?"

"On the contrary," replied Jacob, drawing himself to his full height. "We are hot on the heels of the Plague Doctor."

The innkeeper pushed his face into Jacob's. "Am I he?"

"May we see behind your left ear?" Abby asked.

Granite-faced, he turned to her. "Nay," he replied. "You may not."

When he poured their ales with his back to them, the inquisitors tried to see for themselves, but his tangled hair was too thick around the ears.

"You'll get nought from me," he grunted, slamming the filled tankards on his counter.

Jacob nodded at Kitty as they made their way to the first-floor common room, but the singer looked away and appeared somewhat subdued. *No doubt, the day's unnerving events*, he thought to himself.

Although upstairs was only marginally quieter, the atmosphere was at least less frenetic, and there were tables available.

"I believe we have a gang of sugar smugglers," said Abby, when they had settled in.

Jacob nodded. "Does it connect with the Plague Doctor?"

She shrugged. "I don't know, Jacob."

"Who do you suppose our murderer is?"

Abby supped her ale, savouring the tepid liquid on her tongue. "I have only theories at present."

Jacob raised a finger. "What was it Hedges told us in Bradshaw's warehouse? 'Word on the docks is Trevelyan became an assassin for hire'?"

Abby waited for him to continue.

"What if word reached the ear of Lydia Mercer? It might give her reason to contact Trevelyan, despite their past? If she were desperate to rid herself of Wilkes and Drake?"

"You still believe the chandler is responsible for the murders?"

Jacob had no time to reply, as Samuel Pepys plonked himself down next to Abby. Removing his soaked hat and periwig, he ruffled his cropped hair and pushed a sheet of paper into the middle of the table.

"What is it?" Jacob asked, picking it up.

"I discovered it in the office of the Collector of Customs, one Joseph Catchpole, who is lately deceased."

"Aye, sir," Jacob interjected. "Catchpole was shot by the Plague Doctor shortly after our arrival in Deptford. However it was an accident, since the Plague Doctor…"

When Pepys raised his hand for silence, Jacob looked put out.

"Read that letter which I placed on the table, Mr Standish," Pepys said. "You may discover that Catchpole's death was no accident."

Jacob read aloud for his fellow inquisitor's benefit.

Letter of Immunity

To Humphrey Wilkes, Able Seaman of the Venturer,

This document certifies that Joseph Catchpole, Collector of His Majesty's Customs, grants immunity from prosecution to Humphrey Wilkes regarding any past smuggling activities aboard the Venturer.

In exchange for this immunity, Humphrey Wilkes agrees to fully disclose the identities of his fellow smugglers and to testify against them in a court of law. This agreement is binding upon the signature of Humphrey Wilkes and ensures his freedom from legal sanction for his cooperation.

Joseph Catchpole

Collector of Customs

"You will note," said Pepys, "that the letter is not signed by Wilkes. Indeed, it was never delivered. On account of the poor fellow's murder, we must assume, at the hands of this despicable Plague Doctor."

Abby spoke up. "Master Pepys, do you believe that Catchpole was murdered, having discovered the sugar-smuggling operation aboard the Venturer?"

Pepys set his glinting brown eyes on hers. "*Do you*, Abigail Harcourt?"

Chapter Twenty-Seven

A Telling Clue

J acob was appalled to find Arthur's mother once again on breakfast duty.

"Have you heard?" she asked as they entered the tap-room bleary-eyed.

"Heard what?" asked Jacob.

The old woman glared at him silently, raking out her ear with her little finger.

"Heard what, Mistress Hall?" Asked Abby.

"That the charlatan Mercer woman is dead. And not a moment too soon."

The night's storm had abated, leaving only brooding clouds. When the inquisitors arrived at the chandlery, there was a small crowd gathered outside, and there were two guards at the door with their swords drawn. They could make out the elegantly attired figure of Samuel Pepys through one of the shop's windows.

Jacob pointed at the door as they entered. A cross and the dreaded slogan had been daubed on it in black. "The Plague Doctor claims another victim," he said quietly.

Without warning, Pepys was upon him, in a distinct lather. "Mr Standish, the Plague Doctor has claimed another victim!" Catching himself, he added in a lowered voice, "This is most embarrassing. Where were my inquisitors? My reputation is at stake."

Jacob, mouthing a wordless reply, adjusted his periwig.

Abby stepped in. "Master Pepys, sir, would you show us the unfortunate woman's body?"

"Aye, aye," he replied distractedly. "'Tis here."

Lydia Mercer lay mere feet away, in an aisle between shelves of nautical supplies. Items from the shelves - nails, hooks, chains, tools - lay strewn about. Signs of a struggle, the inquisitors noted.

The chandler was lying on her back in a cream-coloured nightgown, with a knife wound in her stomach. A man in a long black coat and billowing white shirt was kneeling over the body.

"Are you the physician?" Abby asked.

"Tobias Mace," he replied without looking up. "I am the medical officer at Deptford."

"Is this how she was discovered?" Abby asked.

"Aye," Mace replied.

"Hands in her lap, and her hair neatly combed?"

He nodded.

She pointed towards the entrance door. "Was the lock forced or broken?"

"You would have to ask the guards. I am the physician here, not the locksmith."

Jacob nodded to Abby and went to investigate.

She continued, "Have you discovered anything unusual, sir?"

The physician broke off from his inspection and looked at her. *He's rather handsome*, she thought to herself, *and younger than I might have expected for one of his profession.* He was clean-shaven with chiselled features, paler than the average Deptford denizen, and his dark hair was tied back with a red ribbon.

"You are…?" he enquired.

As she introduced herself and Jacob, her fellow inquisitor returned. "The lock was not forced, nor was the door broken," he announced. "A passing dockworker heard a commotion and came to investigate. He saw a man dressed in plague-doctor garb who appeared to be searching for something. Upon being discovered, he fled through the back door. The dockworker found Lydia Mercer lying there. She was dead."

Pepys spoke up. "She knew the assailant?"

"Did you wish to know my findings?" Mace asked sharply.

"Aye, if you please," said Abby.

Gently, Mace pulled up the right sleeve of Lydia's nightgown to reveal her elbow, which was bruised. "See here, a large bruise."

"Did it result from the struggle here?" Abby asked.

"Nay. It is partly faded, which suggests it was sustained perhaps two or three days ago. Furthermore," the physician lifted Lydia's left hand and took something from it, which he held up, "clasped in her hand I discovered this gold ring, which has a garnet set inside it. Notice that gold rings adorn each of her fingers, except...," he paused, lifting her ring finger, "this one."

"Did her murderer place the ring there?" Jacob asked.

"I do not believe so. The victim's fist was clenched when I arrived, and stiffened, which suggests she died in the early hours of this morning. I believe she herself removed the ring and held it there as she succumbed to her injuries."

"A clue to the murderer's identity?" Pepys wondered aloud.

Abby shot him an irritated glance, which he did not catch. "Yet her hair, so neatly combed," she pointed out, "and her hands, carefully arranged in that manner?"

"Aye," Mace replied, replacing the ring in Lydia's hand. "I believe they were the handiwork of your so-called Plague Doctor."

"Is there a symbol inked behind her left ear, sir?" she asked.

The physician regarded her quizzically.

"If you would be so kind?" she added.

Mace lifted Lydia's head, turned it to one side, and pushed her hair away. "There is not."

Abby rubbed her cheeks and moaned lightly.

"What is it?" Pepys asked.

The inquisitor shook her head. "A heavy unease weighs upon me, sir."

"Then pray tell!"

Abby exhaled loudly. "I believe the Plague Doctor I pursued, who shot Joseph Catchpole, was Lydia Mercer."

The accusation lingered in the air.

The young inquisitor continued, "Lydia is… was left-handed, as we can see. When I recall the scene, I see the Plague Doctor I pursued aiming the pistol with their left hand, which is unusual. She fell hard against a wall while fleeing and clutched at her right elbow in pain. We have observed Lydia's bruise."

Jacob spluttered. "Surely, it cannot be a woman who…?"

"Jacob, she confessed to you that she was the Plague Doctor!" Abby pointed out. "Remember she challenged you to prove it?"

"Aye, but I thought…" he trailed off as the truth of her words sank in.

It was Pepys who addressed the glaring issue. "If this Lydia Mercer was the Plague Doctor, *then who did murder her?* And daub that black cross upon her door?"

Two men appeared; one asked if they could remove Lydia's body, since it was causing a rabble to gather outside.

"Aye," Mace replied. "Carry it to my office, where I shall examine it further."

Pepys and his inquisitors stood stiffly, heads bowed, as one man took the shoulders and the other the ankles of the chandler's lifeless form and lifted it. As they did so, something rolled out from underneath.

It was a hook, such as an amputee might wear in place of a hand.

"Trevelyan," Jacob gasped.

Chapter Twenty-Eight

Plans

Pepys and his inquisitors had much to discuss as they made their way back to the dockyard. Often, the older man had to stop and mop his brow, as he struggled to keep up with Jacob. "Do you honestly believe we have two Plague Doctors?" he asked, puffing. "The chandler and Trevelyan, who does remain at large?"

Abby had become used to matching her fellow inquisitor's long strides, walking quickly like a child accompanying her father. She had grown to enjoy the sensation. "I suspected there may be two," she told the two men, "however I had no proof. Maggie Wilkes reported that her husband's murderer walked awkwardly, as if with a limp. As did you, Jacob, when you pursued your own assailant to the Great Storehouse. It made me doubt my own conviction, that the Plague Doctor I saw could move freely. Now I know I wasn't mistaken.

"We have two murderers, one who moved freely – being Lydia Mercer, who shot Catchpole – and another, who walks with a limp, who killed Wilkes and now Lydia herself."

"If it is Mercer and Trevelyan, then why would they be in league together?" Jacob asked. "He loathed her, and she lived in fear of him."

"And he'd not been seen in Deptford until yesterday," Abby added. "I concur, Jacob, it makes no sense."

"Nor why the woman was stabbed. The Plague Doctor uses a pistol."

"Indeed, Jacob. I'm certain she knew her murderer and allowed him entry without question. Hence neither lock nor door were damaged. The fight between them took place at close quarters, when a pistol would have been useless."

Pepys had fallen way behind. "Hold!" he gasped. "Hold, pray."

The inquisitors waited for him to catch up.

When he had regained his composure, Pepys told them, "It does strike me that this blackguard, Trevelyan, must be apprehended at the earliest opportunity."

Abby glanced at Jacob. "Sir," she said, "I would counsel caution in the matter. It may well be that Trevelyan isn't the second Plague Doctor. Jacob and I, we…"

"Are known to make errors of judgement, Abigail!" Pepys cut in. "Might I remind you of Arthur Hall, *the topiarist*, whom you believed to be some sort of pirate?"

She shrank visibly; Jacob adjusted his periwig.

"I am mightily disappointed in you both," Pepys added. "When I came to Deptford, I expected you would have apprehended the miscreant. Instead, he strikes again! Under your very noses!"

Jacob kicked at a stray wood splinter with his scuffed boot. "Sir, may I…"

"I have not finished, Mr Standish! I placed my trust in you, and yet this foul devil, Trevelyan, prowls Deptford, murdering at will! What do you say to that, sir?"

"I believe I know where he is, sir," Jacob replied, unable to look his mentor in the eyes.

"You do?"

"Aye, sir. Those breadcrumbs I noticed aboard the Venturer. It strikes me now that they were not stale. I was foolish not to investigate them more closely at the time, but I did not…"

Pepys interjected impatiently, "Trevelyan is aboard the Venturer?"

"That is my contention, Master Pepys. It would honour me greatly to accompany you in apprehending him. May I suggest we take a band of the navy's finest armed men with us?"

Pepys clasped Jacob's hand, beaming. "I was hardly planning to arrest the brute myself, Standish!"

Chapter Twenty-Nine

Denial

A band of seven men and Abby made their way, as furtively as possible, down the steep wooden steps to the hold of the Venturer. Jacob led the way with a lantern, closely followed by five naval infantrymen from the Maritime Regiment, with their muskets ready. Pepys held back with Abby (to ensure she came to no harm, he told her).

They stopped at the hidden door to Kitty Blake's hideaway. The barrels were arranged as Pepys and Jacob had previously left them, stacked against the sides of the hold. No light shone through the ventilation holes secreted within its front wall, which suggested that no one was inside. Indeed, the scene appeared precisely as they had left it.

Am I wrong about this? Jacob wondered, trying to maintain a confident exterior. Then he noticed it. The knot in the wood that allowed the hidden door to be opened…

He had replaced it the previous night, yet now it was missing.

He nodded to the marines, whose leader motioned for him to stand aside. When Jacob looked pained and shook his head, the lead marine pushed him back with the tip of his fixed bayonet. Reluctantly, he complied.

It was all over in seconds. In truth, Henry Trevelyan put up no fight. Three, he could have taken; four, at a pinch. Five armed, well-trained men in that confined space... Nay.

His arms were bound behind him, and he was led away at bayonet-point. The inquisitors noticed that his hook was in place. *Does he keep spares?* they wondered.

"You shall swing for this, Trevelyan," Pepys said, when Henry was a safe distance away.

The Cornishman stopped and turned. "Swing for what crime, sir?" He was broad and muscular, with a handsome, care-worn face. Yet, Abby felt sure, his heart was black.

"You are the Plague Doctor sir," Pepys stated.

Henry looked amused. "I am no physician."

"Not *a* plague doctor," Pepys replied impatiently. "*The* Plague Doctor."

"I know not of whom you refer, sir."

Before he could stop himself, Pepys had marched up to confront Trevelyan. "You did murder Humphrey

Wilkes, Joseph Catchpole and lately the chandler, Lydia Mercer, Henry Trevelyan," he said. "And you shall swing for it."

Henry furrowed his brow. "Lydia Mercer, the plague doctor? Is she dead?"

"Do not play games with me, sir!"

In a calm voice, Henry replied, "Sir, Lydia Mercer tended to me when I was gravely ill. I would wish only to thank her for her kindness. If anybody believed I would harm the woman, they were sorely mistaken." He cracked a wry smile. "Nay, I came to Deptford to kill the man who blackmailed me and betrayed me to the Admiralty – the man to whom I gave my spoils yet still he destroyed my career. Alas, it appears, I have failed to crush his bitter heart."

Abby could not help but notice that he did not sound terribly defeated.

"Take him away!" Pepys told the marines. "I shall see this matter concluded with the greatest of haste. Summon the Master Shipbuilder and we shall gather to hear the damning evidence against Henry Trevelyan, whence he will be tried at the assizes by a magistrate."

Abby addressed her master. "Sir, may I suggest we gather at Lydia Mercer's chandlery?"

Although Pepys looked puzzled, he acceded to her wish, setting a time for the inquest at five of the clock that afternoon.

Abby had another request for Pepys. "Do you have the wage ledger for the Venturer in your possession?" she asked.

"I do, Abigail. Why do you...?"

"I request that you confirm a small detail for me."

Chapter Thirty

Maggie Wilkes

The inquisitors visited the home of Humphrey Wilkes's widow, while Pepys busied himself with the arrangements for Trevelyan's arraignment. Before they parted, Abby also requested that her master ensure other members of the Venturer's crew were in attendance.

As they reached Upper Water Gate on the way to Maggie Wilkes's house, Jacob remarked, "It feels like an age since we first passed this place, though it has only been a matter of days."

When Abby did not reply, he nudged her. "I said..."

She gasped. "I beg your pardon, Jacob. I was lost in thought."

"Our time in Deptford has flown."

"Aye," she replied. "An inquisitor's work is all-consuming, I'm discovering, but I wouldn't miss it for the world. Doesn't it make you feel alive, Jacob?"

They reached the dilapidated row of housing where Wilkes's widow lived. "Indeed, I feel the same," Jacob replied after a long pause. "Naturally, I do. I owe Mr Pepys a great debt of gratitude. He has provided for me a purpose in life that I find invigorating. However... this place unsettles me. Deptford brings back ill memories of my days in Woolwich, which I would prefer to forget."

Maggie Wilkes's house came into view, up ahead on their right. Abby stopped. "Henry Trevelyan is not the Plague Doctor. I believe I know who is."

Jacob went to speak, but she stopped him. "However," she said, "if Trevelyan is 'Hook-Hand', as I believe – who started the terrible fire in London – then he should pay for the heinous crime."

"We have no proof that it is he."

"You worked among seafarers. How many wore a hook in place of their hand?"

"I cannot recall any," he confessed.

Abby raised her eyebrow.

Jacob set off again. "You will never prove it."

The inquisitors were heartened to see that Maggie Wilkes had papered over the black cross and slogan on her door. Yet when she appeared, she looked more sallow and weary than before.

Her baby girl, Emma, was asleep on the bed, wrapped in a thick blanket. As they entered, Maggie held a finger to her lips. No fire was lit, and the room was so cold that their breath billowed in clouds.

"What do you want?" she asked.

"We shan't detain you for long, I promise," said Abby. "I must know: did your husband have a symbol inked behind his left ear?"

Maggie blinked rapidly. "How did you know?"

"An educated guess. What was the symbol?"

"It was a black bird. A raven, I think."

Abby smiled. "I'm much obliged to you. One final question, Maggie. You told us the chimney was blocked when we were last here. Is the sweep still yet to arrive?"

"Aye, this house is mighty cold," Jacob added, glancing towards the baby.

Maggie shifted uneasily. "Aye, the sweep is… busy," she replied hesitantly, glancing around the room.

"I thought as much," said Abby. Walking to the fireplace, she stepped inside it and reached up with her right hand, feeling around. "Ah," she said.

Shortly, four small, bulging hemp sacks had been laid in front of the fireplace. "Sugar, I assume?" Abby asked.

Maggie threw herself at the inquisitor and clutched her hands. "Please don't tell anybody!" she urged, then hushed her voice as the baby stirred. "I have never sold it, since I knew not how. I will return it, I swear."

Abby squeezed her hand. "Fear not, Maggie, we shall say nought. Mr Standish will assist in finding a buyer for your sugar."

Jacob looked aghast.

"Won't you, Mr Standish?"

He saw that baby Emma had woken up and was staring at him with wide, blue eyes.

Chapter Thirty-One

Inquest

As Abby and Jacob made their way towards Mercer & Sons chandlery, they saw a familiar figure heading in their direction. It was Robert Drake. When he saw the inquisitors, he rushed towards them, stopping just short of an embrace.

"Is the news true?" he asked eagerly. "The Plague Doctor has been unmasked and taken into custody?"

"Aye, Mr Drake," said Jacob. "You are indeed safe from his clutches."

Drake shook his head in disbelief. "Is it true what I hear? That the Plague Doctor was my former captain on the Venturer, Henry Trevelyan?"

Abby spoke up. "Mr Drake, an inquest is being held at five of the clock in Mercer & Sons, presided over by the Master Shipwright. You would do well to attend."

Drake bowed. "I shall indeed!" he replied. "I am most grateful to you. And to you also, Mr Standish. You have proved to be adept inquisitors and a credit to my friend,

Mr Pepys." With a final nod to each of them, he hurried away.

Abby and Jacob arrived early at the chandlery and were already present when Pepys arrived with Theodore Penn. The Master Shipwright was dressed for the official occasion, in a fine doublet of dark wool, with brass buttons and elaborate embroidery. He wore a long, coiffed periwig and feathered hat. A cream-coloured silk cape and silver-tipped cane added the final touches of authority.

Dockyard workers had cleared an area of the main shop floor by pushing shelving aside.

Gradually, as key players arrived, the scene became set.

Lined up in front of the shop counter, in varying states of unease, were Peter Bradshaw, Arthur Hall, Hugo Hedges and Kitty Blake.

Facing them, seated, were Penn and Pepys.

Among the spectators were Abby and Jacob, Robert Drake, and a number of marines, who had been charged with keeping order.

"Why am I standing here, among these men?" Kitty demanded to know. "I am not the Plague Doctor, assuming that it is he you seek."

"Aye, nor I," said Hedges.

Bradshaw merely smirked; the innkeeper seemed to be enjoying glowering at Jacob.

"Silence!" Penn commanded.

A distant church bell chimed five times, opening the proceedings.

Pepys stood up. "Where is Henry Trevelyan?" he demanded. "How can we hold an inquiry when the accused man is absent?"

Abby stepped forward. She had plaited her hair and looked particularly dignified, even if the outfit Pepys had bought for her was now looking a little shabby. "Master Pepys, if I may…?"

Pepys looked at Penn, who nodded. "Very well," he said.

Abby began, "Master Pepys, I would contend to you, and to the honourable Master Shipwright, Mr Penn, that Henry Trevelyan is not the Plague Doctor. He is guilty, I am certain, of other crimes, but not of the murders of Humphrey Wilkes and Lydia Mercer." She became acutely aware that everyone was staring at her.

Pepys leapt up, spluttering, "This is most improper, Abigail! Can you… can you substantiate this outlandish theory? That Trevelyan is somehow innocent?"

"I can prove who is guilty, sir. And it is not Trevelyan."

Pepys sat heavily. "Then pray do so."

Abby turned to Robert Drake beside her. "Mr Drake, would you join the other persons of interest?" she asked, indicating the row of suspects.

He laughed uncomfortably. "But why? I was a victim of the Plague Doctor!"

Abby looked towards Penn.

"Do as she says, Mr Drake," the Master Shipwright commanded.

The difference in height between those arranged in front of the counter was almost comical, from the hulking Arthur Hall down to Drake, who was shorter than Kitty. They looked across at one another, perplexed. Drake continued to protest and was silenced by Penn.

Abby addressed the Master Shipwright. "Sir, I believe there will be a small inked symbol behind the left ear of many, if not all, of those assembled. May we inspect them?"

When Penn nodded, Jacob stepped forward to perform the inspection.

Behind Bradshaw's ear was the rabbit that Jacob had previously spotted, and behind Kitty's was the crescent moon. Hedges, he discovered to have a fox symbol.

When he stood before Hall, the innkeeper stuck out his tongue. "May I?" Jacob asked.

Hall shrugged, snorting.

Jacob found nothing.

"May I leave now?" the innkeeper snapped. "I have nought interest in their poxy band of smugglers and require no cowardly disguise to confront any fool who wrongs me."

Abby sought Penn's approval and received it. "Aye, you may leave, Mr Hall," she told him.

"This is nonsense!" Drake protested. "Why do I stand here among these miscreants? Bradshaw is the Plague Doctor!"

The pig-tailed sailor turned and grinned at him.

Although Drake resisted Jacob's inspection, the inquisitor was too strong for him. "There is a duck symbol behind his ear," he told those assembled.

"As I suspected," said Abby. "A male duck is a drake, and Drake's nickname is Duck. You saw it in Arthur Hall's gambling ledger, Jacob: 'Duck owes Raven'... How much was it?"

"Twelve pounds, four shillings and... I forget the pennies," he replied.

"A sizeable sum. Which he owed to Humphrey Wilkes. Wilkes's widow, Nora, told us that the design inked behind his ear was a raven, thus we may safely assume that his nickname was Raven. 'Duck owes Raven'." Abby glanced at Pepys and was delighted to see that he looked flabbergasted.

Penn spoke up. "Then Drake killed Wilkes over this debt of money?"

"Nay, sir," Abby replied. "Although it was most convenient, since the gang, including Drake, was running out of money. The sugar smuggling came to an end when their leader, Captain Henry Trevelyan, was jailed on the word of one of his own men. Namely Robert Drake."

Drake exploded with indignation. "I will not stand for this, sir! How dare this serving wench demean my good name! I demand that you…"

The Master Shipwright slammed his cane into the floor. "Silence, Mr Drake!" he bellowed. "Another word, and I shall have you clapped in irons!"

The purser had no choice but to obey. His face was bright red, and he glared at Abby with an expression of pure hatred.

When peace was restored, Penn asked Abby, "If Drake did not murder Wilkes purely for money, then why?"

"'Tis my belief that Joseph Catchpole, the Collector of Customs, became suspicious of the sugar-smuggling operation, having found discrepancies in his ledgers. Master Pepys discovered a Letter of Immunity in his office, addressed to Wilkes. The smugglers found out about this imminent betrayal, since word tends to travel in Deptford, and so both men had to die."

Drake looked fit to burst. Jacob could only shake his head in wonderment.

Abby continued, "Jacob, you bravely uncovered the gambling den at The Ship. What was written on its wall?"

He straightened his periwig. "The words were: 'Roll the dice. Kill or die.'"

"I believe the gang rolled dice to decide who would murder Wilkes and Catchpole." Abby looked at Drake. "Drake lost."

"Then they all knew the identity of the Plague Doctor?" Pepys exclaimed, outraged.

"I cannot prove it, sir, but that is my contention."

Abby went on to explain that Drake had concocted a devious plan to divert attention from his guilt, conveniently doing away with Catchpole in the process. Having killed Wilkes himself, Drake had someone don the same plague-doctor disguise and make it look as though he was the next intended victim.

"Since he had lost the dice throw, his fellow gang members refused to take part. So he resorted to his lover, Lydia Mercer."

"This is a travesty!" Drake thundered.

Penn hammered his cane into the floor repeatedly. "Silence, Mr Drake, we will not hear any more from you!"

Enraged, the purser shouted over him. "I will state my case, sir! She cannot prove any of this!"

Abby motioned to her fellow inquisitor, who walked behind the counter and produced a large, flat, rectangular object shrouded in cloth.

When he returned with it to his place beside Abby, she said, "This is the portrait Lydia was painting ere she was murdered. We saw it when we visited her, and she appeared oddly desperate that we did not see beneath the cloth. Jacob, if you would?"

Kitty Blake's gasp could be heard as Jacob removed the shroud; even Bradshaw's permanent smirk disappeared. The portrait was of Robert Drake, smiling beatifically.

"But I… I… I *commissioned* that!" Drake protested.

"I anticipated you might say that, Mr Drake," Abby replied. "Hence I inspected it earlier. Witness here in the portrait, this heart-shaped locket you hold in your hand. Jacob, whose likeness is set within said locket painted here?"

"Lydia Mercer's!" he announced, thoroughly enjoying himself.

Abby continued, "You will also notice the ring painted on Mr Blake's finger: a gold ring with a garnet set into it. The same ring that we found clutched in Lydia's dead hand. Which you gave to her, along with all the others, Mr Drake, as a token of your affection."

"I did nothing of the sort!"

"Then show us the same ring on your finger, as 'tis painted here."

"Curse you, insolent girl!" Drake cried, and made a break for the door. Within moments, he was apprehended by marines, struggling uselessly.

Abby addressed Theodore Penn. "Mr Penn, sir, Deptford's Plague Doctor is Robert Drake. Not Henry Trevelyan."

Pepys started. "I had all but forgotten that scoundrel amid the excitement. Where is Trevelyan?"

"I set him free, Mr Pepys," Penn replied.

Pepys's mouth fell open. "On the word of whose office, sir?"

"On the word of an office higher than ours."

"The Admiralty?" Pepys spluttered.

Penn shook his head. "Higher than that, sir."

"Old Rowley?"

The two men exchanged knowing glances and fell silent.

Chapter Thirty-Two

Celebration

"Congratulations, Mr Standish!" Pepys said to Jacob, furiously pumping his hand. He turned to Abby, lifted and kissed her fingers. "And to you, Abigail. As a fine judge of character, I knew all along that you both had it in you. Did I not tell you that Robert Drake was a dark horse?"

Neither inquisitor dared point out that he had told them precisely the opposite.

They were in the first-floor common room of The Ship, avoiding the unseemly commotion downstairs. Assuring them that no expense would be spared, Pepys had ordered food and drinks enough for ten. An array of roasted meats - beef, pork and chicken - formed the centrepiece, around which were baked salmon, pease pottage, green salads and a selection of fruit tarts.

Arthur Hall delivered jugs of ale, wine and mead. When he set them down, he addressed a necessarily wary Jacob. "I hate that blackguard, Drake," he told him gruffly. "He stole my family's land and wounded me in the process. These drinks are on the house."

Both men still had questions for Abby, concerning the case.

Pepys went first. "Why did you request that I consult the Venturer's wage ledger?"

"Ah!" she replied, through a mouthful of pie. "I quite forgot. Did Drake receive a pay increase in the last month, as he told his wife?"

Pepys drained a goblet of wine and poured another. "The ship has been in dock for the past three months, since it was damaged by the Dutch whilst returning from Tangier. No man has received a rise."

"As I thought, sir. He lied to his wife to cover for the money he earned through smuggling, and which I believe he also stole from Wilkes after murdering him. I grew suspicious of Drake at the dockyard, when Catchpole was shot. It seemed to me that he looked for the Plague Doctor before Jacob shouted a warning, as if he were expecting him.

"We had met Drake shortly beforehand, and he was most anxious to leave. I believe he and Lydia Mercer set the time for Catchpole's murder at one of the clock. The Customs man's pocket watch was stopped at five minutes past. He was indeed expecting her."

Jacob, who was rather tipsy, nudged Pepys beside him, to the older man's evident irritation. "But Drake has no limp," he pointed out. "The Plague Doctor had a limp."

Abby grinned and wagged her finger at him. "Nay, Jacob. The Plague Doctor had no limp. He wore built-up boots, which were cumbersome to walk in. Drake is so short, he would otherwise have been easily identified."

"Nay!" Jacob exclaimed, slamming the table so hard that his chicken bounced onto the floor. "Were they the same oversized boots that I discovered in the Great Storehouse? Which he had removed to ease his escape?"

Abby nodded. "Remember the footprints in the dust in the back-room of the Plague Museum? One large, one smaller? We thought they were made by two different people. Now I'm certain they were both Drake's: one made by the Plague Doctor's boots, the other by his shoes. He never left Deptford, but hid there all along, with his lover, Lydia Mercer's consent."

"A worthy adversary," said Pepys, hiccuping.

"He certainly tried to cover his tracks," Abby replied. "Dropping that note for you, Jacob, laying false clues to implicate Trevelyan and even his lover, Lydia. Then callously slaying her when he feared she may be persuaded to turn on him. He knew the smuggling gang, who were thick as thieves and equally culpable, would not be for turning. Poor, broken Lydia was less reliable."

"She did not betray him to the Admiralty?" Jacob asked, brushing dirt from the chicken he had retrieved from the floor.

"Nay, that was Drake," said Abby. "When Trevelyan was captured aboard the Venturer, he told us he had come to kill the man - not men - responsible for blackmailing and betraying him. It had to be Drake, since Bradshaw and Hedges are inseparably linked. I paid scant heed, unfortunately, to Kitty Blake's words when she told us she was fed by the bosun while stowed away. Who was the bosun about the Venturer?"

"Bradshaw!" Jacob exclaimed.

"Aye. Trevelyan trusted him to help stowaway Kitty, even though Drake and Wilkes were also part of the smuggling gang. There was a falling out. 'Tis my guess Wilkes lied to his wife that Bradshaw and Hedges were the ones flogged for mutiny, swearing they'd seek revenge. Drake and Wilkes were the mutineers. Drake had his revenge, through blackmail and betrayal."

Pepys lofted a goblet to propose a toast. "To the finest personal inquisitors in all England!"

Abby stared agog at her master. "You refer to me as your personal inquisitor, sir. Am I promoted?" The words caught in her throat as she spoke them.

"Aye, Abigail!" he replied. "You are considerably more useful to me as an inquisitor than as a housemaid. Indeed,"

Pepys paused for effect, "you are a rather ineffectual housemaid!"

How they laughed.

Chapter Thirty-Three

Departure

Pepys borrowed an ornate barge from the Navy Office for their return to Seething Lane, having deemed the occasion worthy of a little ostentation. It was longer than any Abby had seen, with a covered cabin at the rear that was decked in small, colourful flags. She had never travelled in such style and luxury.

Theodore Penn was on the quay to see them off. The previous night, he had seen to it that the members of the smuggling gang were incarcerated, awaiting trial.

Bowing lightly to Jacob, Penn told him, "It appears I was wrong about you, Mr Standish. Clearly your skills lie elsewhere than in numbers. I am much obliged to you, sir." He turned to Abby. "And to you, Abigail Harcourt. You have a fine mind, which I confess does surprise me greatly."

Bowing politely, she bit her tongue.

"My Pepys," he said finally. "We shall no doubt meet again soon."

"Aye, Mr Penn. No doubt we shall."

Abby coughed.

"Ah!" said Pepys, alerted by her. "There is a small favour I would ask of you, sir. The singer… What is her name?"

"Kitty Blake," Abby told him.

"Indeed, the singer at The Ship Inn, whose name is Kitty Blake. Abigail informs me that she provided vital intelligence in the pursuit of the Plague Doctor and is fluent in a dozen tongues. I humbly request, sir, that she be released from jail in recognition of her service to the King and offered the position of translator, in which I am assured she would excel."

"Very well, Mr Pepys, if that is what you wish."

The barge set off upriver, rowed by half a dozen liveried men. Samuel Pepys and his inquisitors settled into their plushly upholstered chairs and smiled at one another.

"Mr Pepys," said Jacob. "What next for your inquisitors? I am eager to begin a fresh investigation, sir."

"Fear not, Mr Standish," he replied, pouring himself a large glass of sack. "I have a case firmly in mind, which will take you to one of London's seamier coffee houses. Your services as my personal inquisitor…," Pepys raised the glass to Abby and lowered his head. "As my personal *inquisitors*, will be tested again soon enough."

***

If you enjoyed reading this Samuel Pepys Mystery, please consider leaving a review on your favourite book site(s) – they genuinely help and are greatly appreciated.

My series link on Amazon: mybook.to/pepys-series

Grab a copy of my free introductory novella, The Samuel Pepys Mysteries Book 0.5: Mr Pepys's Stolen Diaries at ellisblackwood.com.

What's next for Pepys, Abby and Jacob? Read on…

Get the next book...

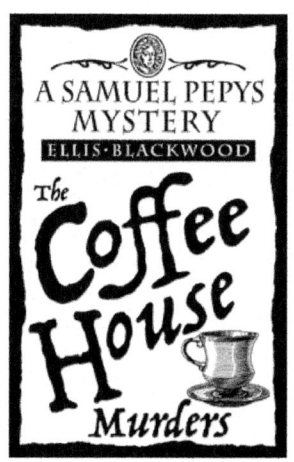

Amazon link: mybook.to/chm-ebook
"Each instalment of this series gets better and better" —
Rambling Mads

Ellis Blackwood

Ellis Blackwood fell in love with the writings of Samuel Pepys, and the 17th-century England he so colourfully portrays, via the great man's published diaries. The Samuel Pepys Mysteries are the result of that literary love affair.

Ellis lives on the coast of Cornwall with his wife, two daughters and dog, Spike. A former journalist, he wrote features for many of the UK's most popular national newspapers and magazines. He recently gained an MA in Comedy Writing from Falmouth University.

The Samuel Pepys Mysteries
Book 1: The Brampton Witch Murders
Book 2: The Plague Doctor Murders
Book 3: The Coffee House Murders
Book 4: The King's Court Murders
Book 5: The Frost Fair Murders

If you've enjoyed this dip into 17th century England – one of the most fascinating periods in England's history – why not join the Pepysaholics? Visit my website to sign up – you'll receive my monthly newsletter, delving into all things Pepys and 17th century, plus the latest Pepys Mysteries news. You'll also receive a **free copy** of the 13,000-word introductory novella, *Mr Pepys's Stolen Diaries*, where we first meet Samuel, Abby and Jacob.

I'm on Facebook and Instagram. Love to hear your thoughts, always happy to answer any questions. Find all my links using this QR code:

Acknowledgements

I could not have published The Plague Doctor Murders without the sterling work of Tim Brown, whose covers are a joy to behold, and whose editorial guidance has been a godsend. Equally, my wife, Sinead, has worked tirelessly and generously in the background to allow me the time and space to write. Thanks also to Charles Johnston, narrator of The Pepys Mysteries audiobooks, for additional editing of the manuscript.

If you'd like to delve further into the world of Samuel Pepys and his navy, I recommend starting here...

- *The Four Days' Battle of 1666* by Frank L. Fox, Seaforth Publishing (2009)

- *The Illustrated Pepys* edited by Robert Latham, Penguin Books (1979)

- *A Journal of the Plague Year* by Daniel Defoe, Penguin Books (1986)

- *London and the 17th Century* by Margarette Lincoln, Yale University Press (2021)

- *Mr Pepys' Navy* by L.A. Wilcox, G Bell & Sons (1966)

- *Samuel Pepys: The Unequalled Self* by Claire Tomalin, Penguin Books (2003)

Printed in Great Britain
by Amazon